JOURNEY TO LOVE

"Why must we travel on to make ourselves unhappy with all we will be facing in Rome? It is so beautiful here I cannot bear to leave it," Shana sighed.

She was speaking more to herself than to the Marquis.

"You are quite right," he responded. "You should never be surrounded by anything but beauty, and that is what I would like to give you."

"The sea," she said dreamily, "the stars in the sky and the moon and of course the flowers. Who could ask for anything more?"

Quite suddenly the Marquis knew that he wanted more.

A great deal more.

Yet he realised it would be a mistake to put his feelings into words.

Even more of a mistake to break the very comfortable and enjoyable rapport there now existed between them.

THE BARBARA CARTLAND PINK COLLECTION

Titles in this series

JOURNEY TO LOVE

BARBARA CARTLAND

Barbaracartland.com Ltd

ISBN 978-1-905155-76-7

Printed and bound in Great Britain by CLE Print Ltd,
St Ives, Cambridgeshire

THE BARBARA CARTLAND PINK COLLECTION

Barbara Cartland was the most prolific bestselling author in the history of the world. She was frequently in the Guinness Book of Records for writing more books in a year than any other living author. In fact her most amazing literary feat was when her publishers asked for more Barbara Cartland romances, she doubled her output from 10 books a year to over 20 books a year, when she was 77.

She went on writing continuously at this rate for 20 years and wrote her last book at the age of 97, thus completing 400 books between the ages of 77 and 97.

Her publishers finally could not keep up with this phenomenal output, so at her death she left 160 unpublished manuscripts, something again that no other author has ever achieved.

Now the exciting news is that these 160 original unpublished Barbara Cartland books are already being published and by Barbaracartland.com exclusively on the internet, as the international web is the best possible way of reaching so many Barbara Cartland readers around the world.

The 160 books are published monthly and will be numbered in sequence.

The series is called the Pink Collection as a tribute to Barbara Cartland whose favourite colour was pink and it became very much her trademark over the years.

The Barbara Cartland Pink Collection is published only on the internet. Log on to www.barbaracartland.com to find out how you can purchase the books monthly as they are published, and take out a subscription that will ensure that all subsequent editions are delivered to you by mail order to your home.

NEW

Barbaracartland.com is proud to announce the publication of ten new Audio Books for the first time as CDs. They are favourite Barbara Cartland stories read by well-known actors and actresses and each story extends to 4 or 5 CDs. The Audio Books are as follows :

The Patient Bridegroom	The Passion and the Flower
A Challenge of Hearts	Little White Doves of Love
A Train to Love	The Prince and the Pekinese
The Unbroken Dream	A King in Love
The Cruel Count	A Sign of Love

More Audio Books will be published in the future and the above titles can be purchased by logging on to the website www.barbaracartland.com or please write to the address below.

If you do not have access to a computer, you can write for information about the Barbara Cartland Pink Collection and the Barbara Cartland Audio Books to the following address :

Barbara Cartland.com Ltd.
Camfield Place,
Hatfield,
Hertfordshire AL9 6JE
United Kingdom.
Telephone: +44 (0)1707 642629
Fax: +44 (0)1707 663041

THE LATE DAME BARBARA CARTLAND

Barbara Cartland who sadly died in May 2000 at the age of nearly 99 was the world's most famous romantic novelist who wrote 723 books in her lifetime with worldwide sales of over 1 billion copies and her books were translated into 36 different languages.

As well as romantic novels, she wrote historical biographies, 6 autobiographies, theatrical plays, books of advice on life, love, vitamins and cookery. She also found time to be a political speaker and television and radio personality.

She wrote her first book at the age of 21 and this was called *Jigsaw*. It became an immediate bestseller and sold 100,000 copies in hardback and was translated into 6 different languages. She wrote continuously throughout her life, writing bestsellers for an astonishing 76 years. Her books have always been immensely popular in the United States, where in 1976 her current books were at numbers 1 & 2 in the B. Dalton bestsellers list, a feat never achieved before or since by any author.

Barbara Cartland became a legend in her own lifetime and will be best remembered for her wonderful romantic novels, so loved by her millions of readers throughout the world.

Her books will always be treasured for their moral message, her pure and innocent heroines, her good looking and dashing heroes and above all her belief that the power of love is more important than anything else in everyone's life.

"Whenever I hear that wonderfully romantic song 'Three coins in the fountain', I fondly remember throwing a silver coin into the sparkling waters of the Trevi fountain in Rome, making my wish for love and of course my wish did come true."

Barbara Cartland

CHAPTER ONE

1885

Lord Hallam was leaving for London and the whole house was in turmoil.

He had been one of the most successful Secretaries of State for Foreign Affairs that England had ever produced.

He believed that when he retired and moved to the House of Lords he would no longer be concerned with diplomacy. However whenever there was a crisis in foreign parts, invariably he was called back to duty.

As he was an extremely active and intelligent man for his age, he could not refuse.

What he disliked most was leaving his daughter, Shana, alone in their country house.

There were plenty of relatives who would have been only too willing to come and stay with her, but when her father was not at home she preferred to be on her own.

"I find them such a bore, Papa" she told him, "after being with you. If they are my female relations they talk and talk about how wonderful it was when they were young and that is of no interest to me at the moment."

Her father had laughed.

"Of course not and I promise you, my darling, that as soon as my book is finished we are going to London. I will give you a ball and you will undoubtedly become the *debutante* of the Season."

Shana thought she would be rather an old one as she was already nearing nineteen, but she did not want to upset her father by saying so.

She was perfectly happy in their charming house in Hertfordshire. They had many well-bred horses to ride and a large acreage of land to cultivate and there were woods which she found entrancing.

The garden was always a blaze of flowers while in the winter they flourished in the greenhouses.

Shana had been born when her father was an older man than most bridegrooms. He had been late in marrying because his political work kept him so busy.

He had thought when finally he fell in love with the daughter of the Duke of Larington that he would have a large family.

Unfortunately his wife, who was a widow, could only produce one child. It left her in such ill-health that she died when Shana was only fifteen.

Lord Hallam then devoted himself to his daughter and she adored him.

Because she had inherited her father's brain, she was able to help him work on his autobiography and his voluminous correspondence.

Shana loved assisting him in the mornings and she would help to supervise the farms on the estate working for many hours in the large library.

The last thing Lord Hallam wanted at the moment was to be asked to go abroad again.

Yet when the Prime Minister, Mr. Gladstone, went down on his knees to beg him to go to Paris on an urgent diplomatic mission, he found it impossible to refuse.

"I will be back as soon as I can," he said to Shana as the carriage came to the door.

"Take care of yourself, dearest Papa," sighed Shana, "and do not stay up too late at night."

Lord Hallam groaned.

"That is inevitable. There is no one who can talk more than the French and they become even more voluble when it is dark than they do in the daytime!"

They both laughed and then Shana saw her father into his carriage, which was a large and exceedingly comfortable one.

She was just about to shut the door after kissing him goodbye when he bent forward,

"Do not forget to give old Bob the tobacco I left for him. I know he is looking forward to it."

"I won't forget," Shana promised.

She closed the carriage door herself although there was a footman waiting to do it and waved until her father was out of sight.

With a deep sigh she walked back into the house.

There were beautiful flowers in the hall and vases filled with them in the drawing room. The mere sight of flowers always made her feel happy.

She told herself that while her father was away she would have more time to spend in the garden.

She would miss him so much, but at the same time the old servants who had been with her family for years would look after her.

She had grown used to being alone.

She was, in fact, quite honest when she said that she

did not really enjoy being with other people. Anyone looking at her would have thought it was an extraordinary statement from a girl who was so beautiful.

Her mother had been a beauty in her time and her father was a very handsome man. It was therefore not surprising that Shana had inherited much of their looks.

Perhaps Fate had added the rest.

Her hair was her most unusual feature.

Although it was very fair there were touches of gold which shone in the sunshine, sometimes in a way that was almost blinding for those looking at her.

Her eyes should have been blue, but instead they were the green and gold of a spring which ran through the gardens and into the small lake at the far end by the wall.

She had a small heart-shaped face.

There was something about Shana which made her stand out, not only from other girls of her age, but also from women who were much older.

She loved reading and could play the piano extremely well.

She enjoyed above all the discourse and arguments she had with her father. They discussed everything new which appeared in the newspapers and everything old in the history books.

One activity they especially enjoyed together was finding some new volume for the family library, which had been started by Lord Hallam's great-grandfather and added to by every succeeding generation.

The Hallams had originally lived in Huntingdonshire and then conveniently, as far as the present head of the family was concerned, they had moved to Hertfordshire so as to be near to London.

It was certainly a blessing for Shana's father as he

could leave his office in Whitehall and drive to the country in about two hours.

*

'Now what shall I do?' Shana asked herself and then she remembered the last words her father had said to her.

Bob Grimes kept an ancient Public House in the small village which lay at the bottom of their drive. He was now an old man and had known her father ever since he was a boy.

Lord Hallam thought it rather touching that he admired him so overwhelmingly and he never forgot his birthday or any other anniversary which occurred during the year.

Even if his Lordship was in some foreign parts, a card would come from Bob Grimes. His name would be scrawled rather untidily at the bottom of it as he could not write very well.

When he took over the Public House called the *Rose and Crown* it had been his wife who had managed everything for him and she had made it very much more attractive to casual visitors than it had ever been.

It was possible, thanks to Mrs. Grimes, for customers to partake of luncheon or supper at the *Rose and Crown* and when there was a wedding in the village there was nowhere else where the reception could be held.

'I will go and see Bob at once,' Shana told herself.

She knew the old man would be very interested to know, if he had not been told already, that her father had gone abroad again.

It was a lovely day despite the fact that it was the beginning of October and Shana did not need a heavy coat and was warm enough in the dress she was wearing.

One of her father's dogs who would never leave his side attached himself to her and they walked down the drive of ancient oak trees.

She was carrying the tobacco which her father had brought down from London. He often gave some to old Bob when he remembered.

It was a special tobacco that could not be bought in the village and Bob would enjoy every puff of it in his large pipe.

Shana walked through the lodge-gates which were both occupied by pensioners who had once worked on the estate and it was just a short walk to the beginning of the village.

First there were just the thatched cottages, some of them black and white which were very picturesque and next there was the shop which had for sale almost everything that anyone could want.

On the other side of the road there was the village Church, which had been there since Norman times and a little further on was the village green.

Facing it was the *Rose and Crown* which was also a delightful black and white building with a tiled roof and a large stable yard at the rear.

There were only a few people about at this hour of the morning, as the men would have gone to work and the women would not yet have started their shopping.

Shana had to wave to only a few women in their cottage gardens as she walked across the green with the dog running ahead of her with his nose down.

The door of the *Rose and Crown* was open and she walked straight in.

There was no sign of anyone in the bar so she looked in the dining room, where she saw that a large table had been laid out in the centre of the room.

She wondered who it could be for.

Then thinking Bob and his wife must be in the kitchen, she walked in to find Bob standing at the stove in which only a small fire was burning.

He turned round as she entered and exclaimed,

"Miss Shana! I didn't expect to see you."

"I have brought you a present from my father. It is the tobacco you like so much."

"That's so kind, very kind. But I don't know what to do, Miss Shana, and that's a fact."

"Why, what has happened?" Shana enquired.

She noticed as she spoke that he looked very harassed.

The few grey hairs he had left were standing up on his head and he was not smiling happily as he usually did.

"It be the missus," Bob told her.

"Why, is she ill?"

"Her's broken her leg, Miss Shana. Her fell down the stairs and we had a job, I can tell you, getting her up again."

"I am so sorry to hear this," Shana sympathised. "And of course I will go and see her."

"I thinks her'll be asleep after what the doctor gave her to stop the pain. But I don't know what to do without her."

"I see you have a large table out in the dining room," Shana remarked. "Have you a party coming today?"

"I have indeed," Bob replied. "And who's to cook for 'em, I'd like to know. I've promised 'em a good meal and how am I goin' to keep me promise without me wife?"

"Surely there is someone who can come in her place," Shana asked.

"Not to cook the sort of food his Lordship requires," Bob answered.

He made a sign of anguish before he continued,

"I were so proud when he comes here a few days ago

and asks if he can bring his shootin' party for luncheon! 'Of course, my Lord,' I says, 'it'll be a privilege to have you.' He told I what he wants 'em to eat, and the missus and I were as pleased as punch to think us'd have 'em under our own roof."

"And who is your guest?"

"The Marquis of Kilbrooke," Bob replied on a note of triumph. "I never thinks he'd be wantin' to come 'ere. But then 'is father never shot this end of the estate. I thinks it be too far for 'em to go back to the Hall for luncheon."

Shana now knew who was coming and was almost as impressed as Bob.

The Marquis of Kilbrooke had only recently inherited the title after his father's death and his magnificent house was about four miles away from the village.

Shana's father had of course known the previous Marquis, who had been ill for many years before he died and she had not been to Brooke Hall since she was a small child.

She remembered it was enormous and had thought that anyone who lived in it must be a King!

The Marquis's illness, which was a stroke, made it impossible for him to communicate with those around him.

There had therefore never been any opportunity for Shana to see the Hall again and it was only last year, just before Christmas, that the Marquis had finally died.

Now his son had inherited.

She had heard a good deal about the Marquis. He was a man of about twenty-seven, who had been talked about in London and had been the focus of gossip in the County.

He was reputed to be dashing, athletic and handsome.

At the same time, so Shana was told, he was most particular with whom he associated. In fact, to put it bluntly, he gave himself 'airs.'

Her father had met him once or twice and he had thought, although it was on a short acquaintance, that he was extremely intelligent, but he clearly liked having his own way.

Lord Hallam told his daughter they could expect a great many changes locally once the new Marquis had taken over the Hall and the huge estate of many hundreds of rolling acres.

"It is a tragedy that the old Marquis should have lasted so long," her father had said. "But there was nothing anyone could do about it. His son served in the Household Brigade and then, I have heard, travelled a great deal on the Continent."

"Why did he not come down here and run the estate," Shana had asked, "since his father was too ill to do anything?"

"I expect he would have found it very gloomy with a dying man in the Hall," Lord Hallam answered, "and he would feel that he should not make any changes until it the estate properly his."

He paused before he gave a faint smile and added,

"I suspect that when he is in London his time is fully occupied. He is, I am told, a friend of the Prince of Wales and his love affairs are as much whispered about as those of His Royal Highness."

Shana had laughed.

"Then he certainly will have no use for Hertfordshire and us," she said, "so we will just have to forget him."

The neighbours were all agog when the new Marquis finally arrived at the Hall. He had allowed two months to pass after his father's death before he took over.

They learned first that he was travelling abroad and then that he was in London with the Prince of Wales.

When finally they heard he had moved into the Hall, people of local importance waited for an invitation.

But nothing came.

Shana and her father heard again and again from their neighbours how much they resented that there seemed to be no chance of their ever being invited to Brooke Hall.

"I believe already great improvements have been made inside the house," one of their friends said. "And the Marquis holds weekend parties for his London friends. But although I have called on him and so have several other locals, he has not returned our calls nor have we received an invitation to anything."

This created an atmosphere of resentment towards the Marquis.

Shana could not help feeling that he would find the people in the County rather boring and she and her father often sighed when they heard the sound of wheels outside their front door.

They knew that they would be interrupted from their work on his book and instead they would have to listen to a lot of gossip and a pile of complaints – none of which were of any interest or importance.

"If I were the Marquis," she said once to her father, "I would put up a notice saying *not at home* at the end of the drive. Then people would not be so indignant when he refused to see them."

"I suppose we cannot blame him altogether," her father responded. "He is young and you must admit, my dearest, that the people who live around us are not particularly exciting."

He laughed before he added,

"In fact I would much rather talk to old Bob. I find him much more interesting."

Shana had laughed too as she had understood exactly

what her father meant.

Now she was confronted with a very different problem.

She could understand only too well how excited Bob was. He was having the 'mystery man,' which the Marquis had become, eating in his dining room.

It would be an event for the village to gossip about for the next six months.

An undoubted feather in Bob's cap and very good publicity for the *Rose and Crown*.

"There must be someone," Shana wondered, "who can help you."

"Not at this last moment," Bob replied. "The only woman who can cook nearly as well as the missus is workin' in the next village. Her won't be back until late in the afternoon."

"What time are they coming here?" Shana asked.

"His Lordship says I were to be ready for 'em soon after noon. What can I give 'em? With only Winnie here who can't cook an egg without making it as hard as a cannon ball!"

Shana laughed and then said,

"Well, I can see it will just have to be *me*."

Bob stared at her.

"What be you sayin' Miss Shana?"

"I am saying I will cook your luncheon for you, but you have to promise you will not tell him who I am, because Papa and I have not called on him as it is quite obvious he does not want visitors."

"You'll cook the luncheon for me, Miss Shana?" Bob repeated in an awed tone.

"I am considered quite a good cook. In fact I often cook for Papa the favourite dishes he enjoys in France or

Italy."

"All I can say," Bob stuttered, "may God bless you. I've never known such kindness – but I might have expected it from – your father's – daughter."

There was a break in his voice and there were tears in his eyes.

Shana took off her hat and found a clean apron hanging up on the kitchen door.

She learned from Bob what had been ordered for luncheon and saw that Mrs. Grimes had already prepared some of the food as it was ready in the larder.

She told Bob to stoke up the fire and then walked over to the dining room, where she found Winnie, the maid, who was employed by Bob, sweeping the floor.

She was a girl of about sixteen and very stupid.

There was an older one whom he had employed for years. She had unexpectedly married one of his customers and left to live in another village.

Shana showed Winnie how to lay the table and told herself that she would have to go back later to make sure she had done it properly.

Next she returned to the kitchen.

It was really quite a simple luncheon his Lordship had ordered.

There were to be curried eggs to start with, which were already in the pan waiting to be cooked. Next came steak and kidney pudding made with the best meat available and vegetables to go with it and there was cheese to finish the meal.

There were, Shana learned, some excellent wines which the Marquis had provided and they at least could be dealt with by Bob.

She could not help thinking it was rather amusing that

she would be able to see the Marquis at close quarters. Practically no one in the County had even had a glimpse of him.

'He sounds obnoxious,' she told herself.

However, perhaps it would be fairer not to judge him before she had actually seen him.

She thought it would be something most interesting to tell her father about when he returned.

If the Marquis was not aware of who she was, there was no reason why anyone else should know what had happened.

Everything was ready by the time the hands of the clock in the bar stood at twelve noon.

In the last half-an-hour they had heard shots in the distance and it sounded as if they were getting a large bag, which was not surprising as Bob had said this part of the Kilbrooke estate had not been shot over for many years.

A short while later Shana looked out of the window into the yard behind the inn and saw gamekeepers carrying an enormous amount of game.

They were followed by the guns who came into the house by the back door where Bob was waiting to welcome them.

"Good mornin', my Lord," Shana heard him say. "I hope your Lordship's enjoyed good sport."

"Very good indeed," a voice answered. "And I assure you we are all hungry. Is luncheon ready?"

"I thinks you Lordship might like a drink first," Bob suggested. "I've opened the bottles your Lordship brought 'ere."

"Then we will do just that," the Marquis agreed.

He had a deep clear voice, but Shana felt, however,

that there was something a little cold and impersonal about it.

'I am being critical,' she warned herself.

Her father had taught her many years ago to analyse the people she met. She must, he had said, be aware of what they were feeling and not only of what they said.

She had learned to be a good judge of character as her father had always been and he had often told her how useful it was to him in his diplomatic life. He would realise even before a man spoke what his character was really like.

'I am sure the Marquis is stuck-up, just as they have said he is,' she told herself.

She was looking forward to the moment when she would see him.

It was no use trusting Winnie to hand round the food as she was quite certain the girl would make a mess of it.

Therefore when she had finished cooking, she found another clean apron and put it on over her dress. It was good that it concealed the well-cut and quite expensive gown she was wearing.

Her father had always been very particular that she wore clothes which, as he said, 'framed her beauty.'

"Far too many women," Lord Hallam advised, "often think it is unnecessary to make the best of themselves when there is no one to see them or just the family."

His eyes were very tender as he added,

"I want to admire you, my darling, every day we are together, just as much as if you were dressed for a ball at Buckingham Palace or a reception at Windsor Castle."

Shana had smiled, but she knew exactly what he had meant.

She therefore always wore clothes which were elegant and becoming, although there was no one to see her but the flowers and the dogs.

She walked into the dining room after the men had seated themselves and she had no idea that one after another they were looking at her in astonishment.

She offered the dish of curried eggs first to the gentleman on the Marquis's right and then to him.

She could not help giving him a quick glance as she did so.

Shana was surprised to find that he was far better looking than she had imagined he would be. His hair was thick and dark and he had a square forehead and his features were almost classical.

He was laughing at something someone had said to him and he looked young and carefree and not, as she had expected, aloof and fault-finding.

She went round the table.

Only when she had left the room did a guest sitting next to the Marquis say,

"That is the prettiest girl I have seen for a long time. Are there many like her in this part of the world?"

"I haven't the faintest idea," the Marquis replied.

"She is certainly unusual," another man chimed in. "I thought for a moment our host was playing a trick on us and she was a star from the theatre, dressed up as a maid to bewilder us."

"I had not actually thought of anything so intriguing," the Marquis said, "but I will keep it in mind for another time."

They all laughed.

When Shana came back to collect the empty plates, there was almost a silence as she circled round the table.

The steak and kidney pie was cooked to perfection.

One of the Marquis's guests commented,

"You are very lucky, Kilbrooke, to find a pub that cooks as well as this. I had expected, when I was told luncheon was to be held here, that it would be sandwiches and cheese."

"I would not insult you with anything so dull," the Marquis responded. "But I do agree with you, the food is excellent and I shall certainly come here again."

"It is very much more comfortable than sitting under a hedge," one of the others said. "I had to do that last week and I can assure you even a big bag did not make up for the discomfort of it."

They all began to talk about the shooting luncheons they had eaten in different parts of the country.

Then the cheese and the coffee were taken round.

When Shana offered the sugar and cream on a tray to the Marquis, he enquired,

"Have you been at the *Rose and Crown* for long?"

"Not very long, my Lord."

"We have been very well served and I would like to thank the cook and tell her that both dishes were excellent."

"I will convey your message to the kitchen, my Lord," Shana said, leaving the dining room.

When she had gone one of the Marquis's guests remarked,

"I think you should have spoken to the cook yourself. She might come in handy on occasions, one never knows."

"I agree," another joined in. "Good cooks are hard to find in the country and one never knows when one might need one."

"Especially if they look like the young woman who waited on us," one of the others said.

They laughed at this exchange.

Then Bob came in with the excellent port the Marquis

had provided.

He took it round the table and when he had done so the Marquis said,

"We enjoyed your luncheon enormously, Grimes, and I would like to thank your cook before I leave."

"I'm glad to hear your Lordship enjoyed yourself."

"Now I think about it," the Marquis added tentatively, "I believe you told me that your wife does the cooking."

"Her does as a rule," Bob answered. "But her had an accident this mornin' and the doctor had to set her leg."

"I'm sorry to hear that," the Marquis replied. "But how were you so clever as to find someone so good to take her place?"

"I've been thanking Heaven for that meself, my Lord, and that's the truth."

He left the dining room without saying any more.

It was soon time for them to leave the *Rose and Crown* for the next drive and they rose from the table and started to find their way back to the stable yard.

The Marquis stopped at the kitchen door. It was ajar and he could hear voices inside.

He entered to see the girl who had waited on them standing at the kitchen table.

Shana was actually putting some left over food on a tray as she intended to carry it upstairs to Mrs. Grimes.

She had taken off her apron.

The Marquis thought the deep blue of her gown accentuated the translucence of her skin and the striking gold of her hair.

Shana looked at him.

Bob had been sitting on a chair and he scrambled to his feet.

"You'll be leaving now, my Lord?"

"We are leaving," the Marquis replied, "but I wanted, as I told you, to thank your cook for a most excellent luncheon."

There was silence before he asked,

"Is it possible that you not only served the meal, but also cooked it for us?"

He was addressing Shana, but before she could reply Bob piped up,

"I tells you, my Lord, me wife were laid up unexpected like this morning, but an angel comes down from Heaven and I be as grateful as you be for what you has just eaten."

"And I am very grateful indeed. Thank you, I hope we can come here again and you will cook me another delicious meal."

Shana did not reply – she just smiled.

The Marquis turned and walked from the kitchen and as they heard him go out into the yard, Bob said,

"Us can't ask for more than that can us Miss Shana? I be so grateful to you, I don't know what to say."

"You must say nothing," Shana told him, "and tell Winnie she is not to talk or tell anyone in the village what has happened. It would be a great mistake for anyone to know what I have done and I am certain that my Papa would not like it talked about."

She knew that where Bob was concerned that argument would be more effective than anything else.

"I promises you I'll say nothing," Bob assured her. "But if he comes here again he'll be disappointed."

"Nonsense," Shana said. "Your wife is an excellent cook, as we all know. But if the story gets talked about in the County, his Lordship might find somewhere else for his guests to eat."

She thought this idea ought to keep Bob quiet anyway as she climbed upstairs to take the food to his wife and she told Mrs. Grimes that no one was to know that she had cooked for the Marquis's guests.

"I'll see that Bob doesn't talk, Miss Shana," Mrs. Grimes said. "I knows if he thinks it'll upset your Dad he'll keep his mouth shut. His Lordship's his hero and always has been."

"I know that," Shana said, "so just keep telling him Papa would be very angry if he thought I was laughed at for having helped you when you were in trouble."

"You be kindness itself," Miss Shana, "and I thanks you from the bottom of me 'eart."

When Shana left she told Bob if there was anything he or his wife wanted, he was to send someone up to the house.

"I shall be alone now that Papa is abroad, so I can help you in any way I can. But I do hope Mrs. Grimes will be better tomorrow."

*

When she retired to bed that night Shana felt it had all been quite an adventure and the story would certainly be something new to tell her father when he returned home.

She thought the Marquis, when she could see him clearly, was even better looking than she had thought at first. He was well over six feet tall and moved like a man who had complete control of his body.

'He will be a good rider,' Shana told herself.

She wondered if he would condescend to hunt with the rather inferior local pack, which she and her father rode to in the winter.

She rather suspected the Marquis would hunt in Leicestershire and if she was not mistaken he maintained a hunting-box there.

'What it comes down to,' she decided, 'is that Hertfordshire will see very little of him. 'But I do not suppose he will be a very great loss.'

*

The next day she found herself worrying a little more over Mrs. Grimes.

She therefore gave orders for their cook to make her some dishes which could be warmed up. There was a soup which her father always enjoyed and which was very nourishing and it was easy to consume when one was not well.

She put these and several other items into the chaise she habitually drove when she visited the village and drove to the *Rose and Crown*.

Bob was delighted to see her again so soon and he and Winnie had carried the food into the kitchen.

"Now that be just what the missus wants," he exclaimed. "It's no use me tryin' to cook. I never were a good hand at it and Winnie be just as bad. Me missus wouldn't even taste what I takes her up for breakfast."

"We must persuade her to eat," Shana observed, "otherwise she will get weaker and her leg will take much longer to heal."

She climbed upstairs and gave Mrs. Grimes the same message.

"I lies here a-worrying, Miss Shana," she sighed, "as Bob ain't eating anythin' with only that stupid girl to cook for him. The eggs she sent up this mornin' be so hard I needed a pickaxe to break 'em. Heaven knows what her'll give me husband for lunch!"

"Don't worry, I will go down and cook him something," Shana reassured her, "and tomorrow I will bring some more food if you promise to eat up everything I have brought to you today."

"You be sent down from Heaven specially to help us," Mrs. Grimes muttered. "And God'll reward you, I can be sure of that."

Shana walked downstairs to the kitchen to find Bob standing by the stove and there was no sign of Winnie.

"What are you doing?" she asked.

"I be tryin' to heat up this meat for the two gentlemen as has just come in," he answered. "They be foreign chaps and as they orders an expensive bottle of wine, I didn't like to send 'em away."

"No, of course not," Shana agreed. "Let me do it."

She could see that he was making a mess of the meat, but she managed to prepare it so that it was edible. She added a delicious sauce and some vegetables.

She took it into the dining room, as Bob was serving someone in the bar and she could see that the two men at the far end of the room were foreigners. She thought in fact they were either Portuguese or Italian.

She put the meat dish down in front of them and one of them said in a heavy accent,

"Good, we wait long time."

"I am so sorry," Shana said. "But now your meal is here I hope you enjoy it."

They helped themselves without replying.

She left the dining room intending to ask Bob whether she should serve them cheese to follow, but he was busy in the bar.

She went back towards the kitchen and as she did so she realised that she could hear the men talking in the dining room.

There was a small window in the room which opened surprisingly into the passage. The pub was very old and alterations had been made to it down the ages.

This window must originally have looked onto the yard and then for some reason when another room was added the builders left it opening into the passageway.

As Shana stopped opposite the window she became aware that the men were talking in Italian and she could understand what they were saying.

"Now what we have to do, Marco," one of them was saying, "is to get there as soon as it is dark. I have arranged with the servant we have bribed to leave a window open for us. I have a plan of the place here with it marked."

"Yes, I know, I've looked at it already," Marco came in. "What is important, Antonio, is to get to the safe where the silver is kept without being seen."

"I thought of that," his colleague answered. "Our friend will be on guard there tonight. We must not forget to tie him up before we leave."

"Yes, of course, but you are sure he knows where the key is kept?"

"He swears he'll have it for us," Antonio answered. "But just to make sure, we'll take our tools with us. From what I hear the safe is an old one and it shouldn't be difficult to prise it open."

"When we've finished this meal, we'll study the plan of the house again. I suppose there's no chance of anyone hearing what we're doing in the pantry."

"The house be as big as a Palace," Antonio assured him. "And the Marquis sleeps right at the other end and so do his guests. The only ones we have to fear is them as sleep on the ground floor. The butler's so old he's getting deaf. Then there's a footman, but I've told our friend to make him as drunk as a Lord before he goes to bed."

The other Italian laughed.

"You make it sound too easy. To be truthful, I'm frightened we have not thought of everything."

"Leave it to me," Antonio replied. "As I've told you before, this silver be worth thousands and thousands of pounds. All we've to do is to get it to Abramo in Rome."

Shana was listening in horror to their conversation.

One man, the one called Antonio was talking with a rather working-class accent, while the other Italian, Marco, was obviously well-educated and much better bred.

Italian was a language in which Shana was very proficient and she had understood every word.

She remembered her father telling her what a magnificent collection of silver the Kilbrookes had acquired over the centuries.

It would be a disaster not only for them but for England if it was stolen and taken out of the country.

The two men had admitted they had bribed one of the footmen and there was nothing she could do now but alert the Marquis to what was going to happen in his house that very night.

It was something she had no wish to do as it would be a mistake for her to have any contact with the Marquis, who believed she was just the cook at the *Rose and Crown*.

At the same time it would be wicked to allow these two Italians to walk off with such a treasure.

Quickly she moved away from the window.

She was quite certain that neither of the men had the slightest idea they had been overheard. They were sitting in an empty dining room, where there was no one but themselves.

She guessed it would be unwise to tell Bob what she had just heard.

As he came out of the bar she asked him,

"Do your guests in the dining room want a pudding or will cheese be enough for them?"

"Give 'em cheese," Bob suggested. "There's also some fruit in the larder and if they have coffee they've nothin' to complain about."

"I think they are quite happy," Shana told him.

She put the coffee ready and left Bob to take it in to them.

There was cheese and some hot toast which she had made quickly as there were no rolls or biscuits to eat with the cheese.

Then she told Bob she had to leave. He thanked her again profusely and she promised to come back the next day with some more food for Mrs. Grimes.

"If I am not able to come myself," Shana said, "someone will bring it. So do not try to make her eat food it is impossible for her to swallow."

"Thank you, thank you, Miss Shana," Bob said over and over again as he saw her into the chaise.

The groom who had accompanied her had taken it under a tree so that it was in the shade. Shana had not forgotten him – she had sent some bread and cheese out for him while she was cooking the meal.

Now as they drove home she was thinking very seriously about what she should do next.

'I suppose I shall have to go to the Hall myself,' she decided finally. 'It is all too complicated to put down in a letter.'

Equally she felt uncomfortable at approaching the Marquis.

If she told him the truth and how she had stepped in to save Bob, it would be too good a story for him to keep to himself. He would be bound to tell the guests he had brought with him.

In which case it would quickly be talked about all over Hertfordshire and that would certainly annoy her father.

'I must keep up the pretence,' she told herself finally.

She wondered when the Marquis would be at home and she guessed she would be able to see him alone at about six o'clock in the evening.

If she went now he might be shooting somewhere else on his estate.

'If I arrive', she calculated, 'just before they go up to dress for dinner, that would give him plenty of time to take action against the burglary. And he will not wish to talk to me for long.'

She thought she had considered her plan as carefully as her father would have done and she could only hope that everything would go off smoothly.

She ordered a chaise to be brought round at five-fifteen and she deliberately chose the same small, rather old one which she had used when she went down to the village.

There were much better vehicles and horses in her father's stables, but that would not look right for the cook from the *Rose and Crown*, even though she could say she had borrowed a conveyance to take her to the Hall.

'I have to think of every detail,' she told herself. 'Otherwise in trying to save the Marquis from being burgled I shall most unfairly end up in trouble.'

CHAPTER TWO

The Marquis decided that the second day's shoot was not as good as the first.

The bag had been smaller and the birds not so high.

He had taken luncheon from the Hall and had it served in one of the keepers' cottages. He considered that the food had not travelled well and the luncheon they had eaten the day before at the *Rose and Crown* was much better.

When they returned to the Hall, however, his guests thanked him profusely. They said they had two of the best days shooting they had enjoyed for a long time.

The Marquis was about to go upstairs to change his clothes, when as he was leaving the hall, the butler informed him,

"Her Ladyship asked me to inform you that she is in the conservatory, my Lord."

The Marquis did not reply, but there was a frown between his eyes as he climbed up the upstairs.

He had begun to think that Lady Irene was becoming rather tiresome and it was in fact time for him to end his *affaire-de-coeur* with her.

He had, when he first saw her, thought she was one of the most beautiful women he had ever seen. She was a little older than him, having turned thirty and was a widow.

She was the daughter of the Earl of Stanton and had married when she was very young and her marriage had proved most unfortunate. She had been irremediably unhappy until by, for her a stroke of good fortune, her husband was killed in a railway crash.

It would have been hypocritical for her to pretend to mourn for him. She had merely left the country house where they lived and moved to London to enjoy herself.

As soon as she was out of mourning, she started to entertain and to be entertained.

Because she was beautiful, amusing and knew almost everybody of any importance, she instantly became a huge success. In fact it was impossible for any hostess giving a fashionable party not to invite Lady Irene to be one of the guests.

She discreetly took a number of lovers, although it was inevitable that a great many people in Society would become aware of her activities.

As soon as she met the Marquis she was determined to capture him, particularly as everyone had told her how difficult he was and how one beauty after another had failed to attract him.

But Lady Irene was very confident of her charms and she was extremely clever in stalking the Marquis as if he was a wild stag.

It took him a little time to realise that, whomever he dined with, Lady Irene was always in the party. Invariably, because she was of consequence, she had her host on one side of her and the Marquis on the other.

Lady Irene played her cards very cleverly.

Although she saw him practically every night and often at luncheon as well, she was amusing, witty and flattering, but never intimate.

Finally she asked the Earl to dinner only to find that he

was the only guest at her attractive house in Mayfair.

There was no question of how the evening would end and he found her passionate and insatiable.

Afterwards it was impossible, as they were seen everywhere together, for people not to realise what was going on.

Their affair did not create as much of a sensation as it might have done, but at the same time the Marquis knew he was being talked about and he disliked gossip intensely.

Yet when he saw Lady Irene coming towards him, looking so beautiful and dressed exquisitely, he thought it was almost worth it.

When he arranged his first shooting party of the Season in the country, he would not have invited her if she had not insisted on it.

"Of course I must help you entertain," she told him, "and as you know as well as I do that I am longing to see Brooke Hall."

"I have a great deal still to do to the house," the Marquis said, "and I think it would be better if you waited until the alterations are completed.

"If I do not like them they may have to be done again," Lady Irene replied provocatively.

He thought she was joking, but when she came to the Hall, he had the suspicion that she was making notes of everything she would like changed.

There could only be one explanation for such behaviour and the Marquis realised with horror that she wanted to marry him.

He had long ago made up his mind that he had no desire to rush into matrimony, as many of his contemporaries had married only to find that they were tied to a woman who bored them for the rest of their lives.

It was one thing to woo an attractive, charming girl and quite another to find a few years later that she had nothing to offer except her face.

Her conversation would not change with the years.

Being extremely intelligent himself, the Marquis found most people rather stupid.

If he spent a long time with anyone, whether it was a man or a woman, he invariably found them tiresomely repeating themselves. He then realised that he had learned all there was to learn about them and they had then become boring.

When he had a choice and when he was at his Club, he enjoyed being with much older gentlemen. He found them stimulating and extremely interesting.

He knew this to be impossible where a woman was concerned. No matter how beautiful she was, even if she produced the heir he must have eventually for his title, she would bore him.

He could imagine nothing more appalling than having to spend year after year listening to the same stories, the same complaints.

When he talked it over with two or three of his close friends, they agreed with him. Two of them had been married and although they were quite fond of their wives, they were, as the Marquis was well aware, champing at the bit.

A number of his friends had reached a difficult situation as they had found they could not be alone with their wives because they irritated them so much.

"I feel depressed," one of them said to the Marquis, "every time I walk through my own front door. It is impossible for me to have a divorce, so what can I do?"

A divorce meant a major scandal as well as a long

drawn-out law case which would have to be processed through the Houses of Parliament.

The Marquis had thought over his own position very carefully. He would hope and, he almost added pray, that he would find someone he loved and who would love him.

Then he would be eternally happy as happened in the fairy stories.

He laughed at his own imagination, knowing it would never come true!

There was just a chance he would find someone with whom he could have some kind of working relationship, someone he could get along with amicably.

When she became bored she could more or less live her own life and this meant that there was no question of his marrying a girl very much younger than himself and it would equally be extremely difficult to find an older woman who could fit the bill.

What he had no intention of ever considering was to marry one of the acknowledged social beauties. He knew only too well that they were waiting to be unfaithful to their husbands immediately they turned their backs.

And that of course included Lady Irene.

He knew she had enjoyed one affair after another since her husband had died.

That she might want to marry him had not occurred to him.

She was obviously having such a success with so many men that it seemed unlikely she would be prepared to give it all up for one suitor.

Yet he knew as soon as they entered the Hall that he had made a mistake in letting her join him.

Although, as he had said, a great many alterations were to be made, the house was magnificent. It was one of the finest ancestral houses in England, having been redesigned almost entirely by the Adam brothers.

In perfect taste, the exquisite rooms were each breath-taking when one first saw them and the furniture and pictures were the envy of every museum curator.

Because the Marquis's father had been ill for a long time, the social world had almost forgotten Brooke Hall, but he knew from the way his first guests behaved that everyone would be clamouring for an invitation.

Last night when the gentlemen were leaving the dining room, the guest beside the Marquis had stopped and was looking up at a picture painted by Sir Joshua Reynolds of his grandmother.

"That is one of the most beautiful portraits I have ever seen," he said. "You must be very proud of it."

"I am," the Marquis replied. "She was a great beauty in her time."

"That is what Lady Irene was saying this morning," his companion had responded, "and wondering which artist you would find today to paint her."

The Marquis stiffened but his friend continued,

"I gather however she wants to be hung in the drawing room rather than in the passage."

The Marquis said nothing.

Later that night when he went, as was expected, to Lady Irene's bedroom, she was waiting for him. Their love-making was, he thought, even more passionate than it had ever been.

When he was tired and thinking it was time to return to his own room, she said very softly,

"You are so wonderful! How could you be anything else in this enchanting Palace, which we would never want to leave."

The Marquis pretended that he had not heard what she said.

When he finally found his way back to his own room, he realised that he was in a dangerous position. The trap of matrimony which he had avoided for so long was opening just beneath his feet.

If it had been possible, he would have returned to London the next day taking his party with him.

But it was Sunday! And all his guests had been asked to stay until Monday and it would be impossible for him to find any excuse why they should not do so.

It occurred to him that perhaps Lady Irene would try to make some announcement before they left the Hall and those who were staying there, who were all close friends, would be convinced that she and their host were soon to be married.

They would undoubtedly whisper the story around Mayfair.

'What can I do? What the devil can I do?' the Marquis had asked himself as he dressed to go out for the day's shoot.

All through the day the same question kept rushing through his mind – even when he was bringing off a good right and left.

His valet helped him to change his clothes.

Then just as he was about to go downstairs there was a knock at the door.

"It's Dawkins, my Lord."

Dawkins was the butler who had been at the Hall for many years.

The Marquis was brushing his hair in a mirror which hung over the chest of drawers he used as a dressing table and did not turn round.

"What is it, Dawkins?" he asked.

"There's a young lady to see you, my Lord. She says

it's of the utmost importance and she comes from the *Rose and Crown*."

"*The Rose and Crown?*" the Marquis repeated in surprise.

Then he remembered the young woman who had cooked the shoot luncheon yesterday and his friends had thought her surprisingly beautiful to work at such a menial task.

He wondered what on earth she could want with him, unless perhaps there had been an accident to the proprietor or had the money he had left for the luncheon with an extremely generous tip been incorrect?

"Where is this young woman?"

"I put her in the study, my Lord," Dawkins replied. "The guests are all in the blue drawing room."

"I will be down in a moment."

He finished brushing his hair and his valet helped him into the coat.

He knew the rest of his party would still be having tea, a meal he usually skipped.

It was getting on for six o'clock and he wanted to attend to his letters before he came upstairs again for a bath.

He turned away from the chest of drawers, thinking that whatever the young woman from the *Rose and Crown* had to tell him, he could not give her much time.

*

Shana had been worrying all the way to the Hall about what exactly she should say to the Marquis.

Would he believe her?

She knew it was impossible for her not to warn him that his silver was in danger and equally she found her situation extremely embarrassing. Her father would be horrified at her becoming involved in anything that could cause a scandal.

She began to feel that if she was sensible she would forget what she had heard the two Italians plotting and that she could leave the Marquis to fight his own battles.

But she was aware of the outstanding treasures which were housed at the Hall.

The Marquis's silver ranked as a national treasure.

She and her father had often talked of the treasures he had seen in the different parts of Europe he had visited. She remembered him saying that he had seen the famous enamelled salt cellar in a museum in Vienna that had been made for Francis I by the celebrated Florentine Benvenuto Cellini.

She could remember him adding that the only piece of silver comparable with it, also made by Cellini, was in Brooke Hall.

Shana tried to recall the other treasures he had spoken about belonging to the Hall and because she had not seen them, she had not been as interested as she might have been.

At the same time, however uncomfortable for her, it would be wicked to allow treasures of that value and beauty to be spirited away from England.

'There is nothing I can do,' she thought, 'but tell the Marquis what I have overheard and then leave it to him to cope with the thieves.'

It sounded quite easy, but she had an uncomfortable feeling she might become more involved and she must take every possible precaution so that the Marquis would not guess or learn who she was.

She ordered the old chaise to be ready at five o'clock and told the groom who had brought it that she was only going a short distance and would drive herself.

"Very good, miss," he said, "I'll be looking out for you when you return."

"Thank you, Ben, I will try not to be away for long."

She set off, driving herself with an expertise she had learnt when she was quite small as her father had taught her to drive as well as ride. As he was an expert at both she could not have had a better teacher.

She enjoyed being on her own, driving on roads which were unfamiliar but which she knew led to the Hall.

However, she could not help feeling a little nervous and wondered if she was making a mountain out of a molehill, in which case the Marquis could just ignore her.

However, it had seemed very strange that the thieves should be Italians and that they should actually mention the safe in the pantry where, as Shana knew, in most big houses the silver was kept along with any valuable jewellery.

She reached the gates of the drive and was aware that the tips of the iron posts had been newly painted with gold and the urns on either side cleaned.

She had seen the Hall from the outside when she had been hunting and had thought that the lodges and the gates looked somewhat dilapidated, but she could not say so now.

The drive itself was tidy and the first glimpse Shana had of the house was very impressive with the Marquis's standard flying on the roof.

The last rays of the sun were glinting on the large number of windows and in front of the Hall there was a huge lake and the ancient bridge crossing one end of it had been there for centuries.

As Shana passed over it she had a glimpse of a number of swans moving on the still water and some ducks rose at her approach and flew away from the bridge towards the other end of the lake.

It was all in keeping with the beauty of the house and she thought it was no wonder the Marquis gave himself airs when this was his home.

She had made her plans carefully. Instead of going to the front door as she would have done normally she drove to the stables.

She passed under an arch in the cobbled yard and saw a long row of stables which she knew contained the superlative horses the Marquis was reputed to own.

A stable boy came out to meet her as she pulled her horse to a standstill.

"I am calling to see someone in the house," she told him, "and I would be grateful if I could leave my horse with you. I do not expect to be very long."

"That'll be all right, miss."

Shana climbed out of the chaise, hoping that she did not look too conspicuous.

She had chosen one of her plainest gowns which had a short jacket over it and she wore a hat from which she had taken several feathers before she placed it on her golden hair.

She walked to the kitchen door and when it was opened by one of the scullery maids she said,

"I have come to see his Lordship on a very important matter. Will you be kind enough to tell him I am here."

The girl hesitated and then she replied in a somewhat embarrassed manner,

"I'll tell Mr. Dawkins what you wants."

She turned round and Shana followed her, thinking perhaps she would have been wiser to go to the front door. At the same time, if she really was the cook from the *Rose and Crown*, she would certainly have come to the kitchen entrance.

They walked on through what seemed miles of

flagstones until they passed the kitchen from where Shana could hear voices talking loudly and there was a savoury smell of cooking.

Next they passed through a baize-covered door to what she recognised was the front of the house.

"You stop 'ere, miss," the scullery maid said, "and I'll look for Mr. Dawkins."

Shana did as she was told.

The maid hurried away as if frightened at being in a different part of the house from where she belonged.

It was not long before she returned with the butler.

Shana knew from the way he looked at her that he was surprised at her appearance. He had obviously expected someone looking very different.

"I am sorry to bother you," she said, "but I have a very important message for the Marquis of Kilbrooke and as it is so urgent I would be grateful if I could see him for a few minutes alone."

There was a little pause.

Shana knew the butler was wondering if what she was saying was genuine, because of the way she was dressed this might be some sort of joke.

"I assure you," she repeated, "it is of the utmost urgency."

She looked so pretty that any man would have found it hard not to believe her.

"If you'll come this way I'll inform his Lordship that you are here."

It was only when they reached the study that he asked,

"What name shall I tell his Lordship?"

"Tell him it is the cook from the *Rose and Crown* and he will understand," she answered.

She knew by the expression on the butler's face that he was astonished and at the same time curious. He was however too well trained to say anything and he merely left the study closing the door behind him.

Shana looked round her.

She had taken in a great deal of the house as she had come through it. Now she thought the study was exactly what she might have expected. Two of the walls were covered with books, although she was sure that there was a library somewhere else in this huge building.

A Regency desk with its gold feet was in the window and the gold inkpot standing on it was, she could see, a museum piece.

Over the mantelpiece there was a striking portrait of one of the Marquis's ancestors and the other pictures in the room were by Stubbs and other famous artists who painted mostly horses.

Shana wanted to look at them closely, but she felt it would be a mistake to move about as when the Marquis arrived he might think she was prying.

She therefore stood in front of the mantelpiece, which was of exquisitely carved marble and undoubtedly placed there by the Adam Brothers.

There was a very beautiful clock on the mantelpiece and two gold candlesticks, which Shana guessed were seventeenth century as well as two pieces of Sevres china she would have loved to own.

It was quite obvious, she thought, that treasures like these were every burglar's dream.

'I wonder,' she asked herself, 'if the Marquis really appreciates them or just takes them for granted because he has grown up with them.'

The door opened and the Marquis entered.

In his ordinary clothes he looked even more handsome than he had in the tweeds he had worn for shooting.

As he walked towards her, Shana recognised he resented her taking up his time as he should be entertaining his guests.

Because she felt nervous her eyes were very large in her face.

"I understand," the Marquis said as he reached her, "that you wish to see me."

"I have something – to tell you, my Lord," Shana began, "which you will think – very strange, but I believe it is something – you ought to know."

She spoke a little hesitatingly and as if the Marquis realised she was agitated, he smiled before he said,

"Then I suggest we sit down and you can tell me as quickly as possible what has brought you here. I hope it is not bad news of Mr. Grimes or his wife."

Something flashed through his mind. Grimes had said yesterday when he was congratulating the cook that his wife had just had an accident.

Perhaps she was dead and they could not afford to bury her!

Shana seated herself in an armchair and the Marquis sat down on the one beside her.

"Today," she resumed, "there were two visitors to the *Rose and Crown* for luncheon. When I carried the food into the dining room for them, to my surprise they were Italians."

"Italians!" the Marquis exclaimed. "What are they doing in this part of the world?"

"I wondered that myself, my Lord," Shana replied. "And when I left the dining room and walked back down the passage which leads to the kitchen, I heard them speaking to each other through a false window."

She paused for a moment and the Marquis asked,

"You could understand them?"

"Yes, I speak Italian. One of them was saying that he had arranged with a servant of yours he had bribed, to leave a window open as soon as it was dark and he had a plan of the Hall in his possession."

The Marquis was staring at Shana.

"You knew he was talking about this house?"

"I did not know at first, but later he said 'the house is as big as a Palace and the Marquis sleeps at the far end of it'."

"I don't believe it!"

"He had to be talking about the Hall and before that he said, 'what is important is to get unseen to the safe where the silver is kept.' He added their friend would be on guard inside and would have the key."

"That means it will be one of the footmen," the Marquis muttered as if he was speaking to himself.

"That is what I thought, my Lord," Shana answered. "Then the other man said they would also bring their tools with them as he had heard the safe was an old one."

"I can hardly believe what you are saying," the Marquis said. "But you are quite right the safe is old. But I thought with a footman to guard it every night it would be impossible for anyone to take us unawares."

"Someone else they were afraid of was the butler, but one of the Italians said he was an old man and getting deaf and they had told their confederate to make another footman who might be within hearing 'as drunk as a Lord'."

The Marquis smiled as if he could not help himself.

"Tell me what else you heard. Try to remember everything."

"The taller Italian, called Mario, who was obviously

far the better educated," Shana told him, "and I should imagine better bred than the other, said that the silver was worth thousands and thousands of pounds. All they had to do was to take it to – he said a name but I am not quite certain of it – in Rome and then they would fill their pockets."

"What was the name of the place they mentioned in Rome?" the Marquis enquired sharply.

"I have been trying to remember it, my Lord. It was a rather unusual name, but I think, although I would not swear to it, that it was Abramo or something very like that."

"Abramo," the Marquis repeated as if he intended to memorise it.

"I could not stand listening any longer," Shana continued, "in case they became aware of me. So I went to the kitchen and then I knew I must tell you what was going to happen tonight."

"Of course you had to tell me and I am sure you feel as I do that the silver which has belonged to the family for generations is also a treasure of our country. It would be a tragedy for England to lose it."

Shana smiled.

"I thought that myself when I was coming here, my Lord. In fact I wished I had not overheard what was being planned."

"You were afraid at having to tell me?" the Marquis smiled.

"I thought perhaps you might not believe me – it is somewhat embarrassing."

"Then I can only thank you from the bottom of my heart for being so brave and for saving treasures my family has valued for centuries."

"Touch wood, my Lord. You have not saved them yet. I am sure they will not only be very clever but also dangerous."

"What makes you think that?" the Marquis asked sharply.

"There was something about them which made me think they were not the ordinary burglars we are used to in England."

She saw the Marquis was waiting for an explanation and she went on,

"I mean men who are just hungry and want to steal something they can sell to the first pawnbroker they find. I may be wrong, but I thought these men, especially one of them, was somehow a lot more professional than that."

"I am sure you are right," the Marquis said. "Although most burglars would go for a safe, I suspect these Italians would know what is inside mine."

Shana rose to her feet.

"I can only wish you luck, my Lord, in preventing them from robbing you."

"I shall do my best and I expect you would like to be told the end of the story."

"Of course I hope it all has a happy ending, but I have not mentioned anything to Mr. Grimes and I think the fewer people who know about it the better."

"You surprise me, I thought you would expect me to give you a party in the village to show my gratitude."

"I think it important," Shana said in a serious tone, "that no one in the village has the slightest idea that this has happened or that there has been any trouble. And I would be grateful, my Lord, if you would not tell Bob Grimes or anyone else that I am at all involved."

She spoke so seriously that the Marquis, who had also risen to his feet, looked at her questioningly.

"Now you are being mysterious and I have only just realised I did not ask your name. If I come to the *Rose and*

Crown to see you and you are not there, I can hardly ask for the very beautiful young woman who does the cooking!"

He was aware as he spoke that she stiffened and it surprised him.

"My name," Shana replied in what he thought was a cold voice, "is Davis."

"Then perhaps you can tell me, Miss Davis," the Marquis quizzed her, "why, in the middle of Hertfordshire, you are able to speak Italian so fluently that you could understand every word these two men were saying to each other."

Shana had thought of an answer to this question before she arrived.

"I am a teacher, my Lord, and only happened to be in the *Rose and Crown* by chance when Mrs. Grimes hurt her leg."

She crossed her fingers as she spoke.

She was telling a lie and it was something she never did, although she thought her explanation was quite a clever one.

It would also prevent the Marquis from being surprised if he visited the *Rose and Crown* and found she was not there.

Almost as if he was reading her thoughts, he asked,

"Are you thinking of leaving the village in the next few days?"

"I might do," Shana answered.

"Then I hope you will leave an address where I can find you. I might just want a little more information than you have given me already."

"I have told you everything of importance."

"One can never be sure until one can put a puzzle

together and it could be fatal to find two or three vital pieces of information were missing."

"If I do leave, though I see no reason for it," Shana murmured, "Bob Grimes will know where to find me. But I can assure you, my Lord, there is nothing more I can do. I can only hope you will be on your guard tonight and that no one will be hurt."

"That is what I am hoping myself and I must thank you again, Miss Davis, for coming here and warning me."

The Marquis paused before he said in a different tone,

"I can assure you I shall take more care of my silver and treasures in the future than I have done in the past."

"That is sensible," Shana said approvingly. "I only hope for your Lordship's sake that no one will know what has occurred. It might make other burglars decide to visit the Hall for what they can get out of it."

"I know you are telling me once again there should be no talk or gossip about this plot and I promise you I shall do my very best to make sure your wishes are carried out."

The way he spoke made Shana realise that he thought there was something personal in her desire for there to be no scandal.

She moved towards the door and as she did so she thought he was more perceptive than she had expected.

She had an uncomfortable feeling that if she stayed with him much longer he would read her thoughts or know instinctively what she was thinking.

"How did you travel here?" the Marquis enquired as she reached the door.

"I borrowed a chaise," Shana replied, "and I left it in the stable yard in the charge of one of your grooms."

"Then I will have it brought round to the front door."

Shana was about to protest and then she realised he

would consider it polite to see her leave. He would not wish to go through the kitchen quarters himself.

They walked in silence through the long corridors which led to the hall, where Dawkins was on duty with two footmen.

The Marquis sent one of them to the stables.

"Tell them," he ordered, "to bring Miss Davis's chaise round to the front of the house immediately."

Shana thought it was fortunate that she had not brought one of her father's grooms with her as he would have thought it strange that she was using a different name.

While they were waiting she moved out of the open doorway onto the steps which led down to the courtyard outside.

The view of the lake and the park was incredibly beautiful and she thought how lucky the Marquis was to own anything so superb and sublimely lovely.

"I am exceedingly grateful," he said to her.

Shana turned and looked at him in astonishment.

"You are reading my thoughts."

"I knew that was what you were thinking. It is something I can do with some people, but to be honest I do not usually find their thoughts are particularly interesting."

"These thoughts of mine of course were special because they concerned *you*."

The Marquis's eyes twinkled.

"Now you are accusing me of being conceited."

"You have a great deal to be conceited about. I think the Hall, the garden, the lake, the park, and of course the woods are more beautiful than anyone could imagine or dream about."

She spoke as she would have talked to her father and

she did not see the look of surprise come into the Marquis's eyes.

"One day," he said, "you must see the inside of the house and I think you will find it as wonderful as I do."

"I noticed the furniture and the pictures as I came to your study," Shana replied. "I think such a collection is a great tribute to the good taste of your ancestors. It would have been so easy for them just to buy what was in fashion at the time. But I know from what I have seen that they chose what was outstanding for any age."

"That is a compliment I have not been paid about the Hall ever before and it is one of the best and something I shall always remember."

"Then of course you must be very careful," Shana said, "to make sure that your own contribution is just as important."

She was now watching the approach of her chaise and she missed the look of incredulity spreading over the Marquis's face.

The groom leading her horse drew it to a standstill and when she walked down the steps the Marquis followed her.

"Thank you once again and I will try to let you know what happens without anyone else knowing."

Shana did not answer. She just smiled at him as she climbed into the driving seat, thanked the groom and drove off.

She had no idea that the Marquis was watching her until she was out of sight.

He noticed how well she drove and there was something experienced and expert about her he had seldom seen before in a woman.

Then he strode back into the house to make his plans for the evening.

CHAPTER THREE

Shana heard nothing from the Marquis on Sunday.

When she went to Church she prayed that the burglars had been prevented from taking anything, better still, that they had not turned up at all.

If that had happened, the Marquis would think she had invented the whole story! And if they had made the attempt, she felt sure that the story was bound to leak out. It would be a piece of gossip the village would really enjoy.

She next expected to hear from him on Monday, but Monday came and went and there was still no news from the Hall.

She chose to go riding early in the morning and found the woods were, as always, calming, but at the same time inspiring.

She always felt as she rode underneath the trees that they were telling her stories of the past and yet they themselves were vitally alive.

Ever since she had been a child Shana had been attracted by the woods and she remembered when she was very small running away to cry amongst the trees because her nanny had been cross with her.

She was certain there would soon be a note from the Marquis and when there was nothing, she thought he was extremely rude.

He must be aware she was anxious, but then she told herself he was not likely, being so important, to be concerned about what the cook at the *Rose and Crown* felt or did not feel.

'The sooner I forget this whole episode,' she told herself firmly, 'the better.'

Shana sent food to Mrs. Grimes on Sunday and again on Monday, but she did not go to the *Rose and Crown* herself.

Somehow she felt that perhaps the window in the passage had deceived her and she was half-afraid that the Marquis suspected she was using a new way to get to know him, making up a story which would intrigue him.

To try and forget what had happened, she worked very hard on the research for her father's book. He was going back so many years and had visited so many countries and he wanted to be accurate in everything he wrote in his autobiography.

He insisted on every detail being checked and so far Shana had looked through the history books in the library covering France, Italy, Spain and Germany, but she knew there were other countries her father wanted to write about, the most important being Greece.

She therefore spent a long time with the books on Greece to check what he was saying was accurate, when he wrote of his feelings when he first saw the Acropolis and visited Delphi.

He had done so much and had met so many interesting people whose family trees had to be looked into.

Shana began to think he would be the first person in the world to write his autobiography in three volumes!

It was all very absorbing and she knew when her father returned he would be delighted by what she had done.

Because she found it all so interesting, Shana went to

bed very late and the next morning she overslept.

Rose, the maid who looked after her, brought in her breakfast when she rang at ten o'clock.

"We were worried as to what had happened to you, miss," she said. "It ain't like you to sleep as late as this."

"I know," Shana replied yawning, "but I went to bed long after midnight."

"You'll ruin your eyes pouring over them books," Rose admonished her.

"I do hope not," Shana smiled. "At the moment I find my eyes very useful and there is a great deal more for them to do."

It was a lovely day and she thought she would go riding again, so she sent a message to the stables.

When she had put on her habit she decided to go there herself.

There were quite a number of horses being paraded in the yard for her to choose from and finally she chose a bay which she had not ridden for some time. He was one of her father's favourite mounts, but he was very spirited and, as Shana knew, in need of exercise.

She galloped for a long time before the stallion was prepared to settle down and go quietly.

She rode for quite a long way, before realising that if she did not turn back she would be late for luncheon, although it would not matter particularly.

She always told Mrs. Baker, the cook, to give her a very simple meal when she was alone.

"I can't have you starvin' yourself, Miss Shana," Mrs. Baker had said the last time she made such a suggestion.

Shana realised now that, whatever she might have said, Mrs. Baker would have cooked her something delicious.

She therefore turned her horse round and rode back the way she had come, pushing him as hard as she could.

Nevertheless it was half-past one as she rode into the stable yard.

"We was wonderin' what'd happened to yer, Miss Shana," the groom remarked when she arrived.

"I was giving Hercules the exercise he has been lacking now my father is away."

She walked from the stables into the house and found Baker, the butler, who was married to the cook and was also worrying about her.

Because she knew luncheon was ready she walked straight into the dining room without taking off her habit.

As she had expected, Mrs. Baker had provided an excellent meal, in fact there was far more than she really wanted to eat.

She had just finished a cup of coffee when Baker came in to say,

"There's that girl Winnie from the *Rose and Crown*, Miss Shana, who says she wants to speak to you urgently."

Shana put down her cup and rose to her feet.

"Bring her to the study. I hope she does not bring bad news of Mrs. Grimes."

She was well aware that Baker, who liked to know everything, was becoming curious.

Why had Winnie come to the house at such an unusual time and what was her message about?

Shana reached the study first and a few moments later Baker opened the door to say,

"Here's Winnie, Miss Shana."

Winnie came in looking frightened and Shana could tell that she had been running, as she was still a little breathless and her hair all blown about. She had come just as she was in her gingham dress with an apron over it.

Shana waited until the door closed behind Baker.

Then she said in a low voice in case the butler was listening,

"What has happened? What have you come to tell me?"

Winnie seemed to grunt before she replied,

"It be 'is Lordship, 'e's arrived and 'e wants to see you quick."

"What did Mr. Grimes say to him?"

"'E says you was with friends but 'e'd get in touch with you."

"So Bob sent you."

"'E tells I to run as fast as me legs'd carry me," Winnie said, "and to tell you to come real fast."

Shana wondered what could have happened, but realised she could not go to the *Rose and Crown* dressed in her riding-habit.

"Now you walk back, Winnie, and it is very kind of you to come and tell me I am wanted. I may catch you up, but if not tell Bob I will be as quick as I can."

"I understands, miss, and Mr. Grimes said I was not to say where you was or who you was."

"That is quite right," Shana affirmed. "And you are not to tell my butler, my cook or anyone else in this house why I am wanted. Let them think Mrs. Grimes needs me because she is feeling ill."

"'Er were ever so pleased with the food you sent 'er." Winnie volunteered.

"I am so glad. Now go back to the *Rose and Crown* and remember what I have just said."

She was walking towards the door as she spoke and

51

when she opened it, she was not surprised to see that Baker was not far away, not very obviously waiting to see Winnie out.

As Shana walked past him she said,

"Mrs. Grimes wants to see me and it will be quicker if I walk to the *Rose and Crown* rather than wait for the grooms to bring a chaise round."

She did not wait for Baker to reply but ran up the stairs to her bedroom where she changed as quickly as she could into the same plain dress she had worn before.

Then she hurried downstairs, putting on her hat as she did so.

She sped out of the front door and down the steps and could see Winnie in the distance halfway down the drive. She caught up with her just as they entered the village.

"You've been quick, miss," Winnie commented.

"So have you," Shana replied. "Thank you very much for coming to tell me I was wanted."

"Mr. Grimes were all of a dither when 'is Lordship walks in and when 'e tells I to 'urry 'e means *'urry!*"

Shana laughed although it was quite difficult to do so when they were both walking so quickly.

It seemed to her the village green had never been so heavy beneath her feet, nor the *Rose and Crown* so far. She walked in through the front door as it would have taken longer to walk round to the back.

Bob had obviously been looking out for her and met her as soon as she passed through the door.

"His Lordship be in the dining room," he told her. "There be no one there and 'e wants to talk to you right away."

He was obviously consumed with curiosity as to what it could all be about.

Shana just smiled at him and walked into the dining room and Bob closed the door behind her.

She noticed that the Marquis was sitting at the far end of the room where the Italians had been seated.

He rose as she entered to greet her.

"I am sorry to disturb you, Miss Davis, but it was important for me to see you at once."

Shana walked towards him and said,

"I think we would be wise to sit at the other end of the room. There is the window through which I heard the Italians talking."

She pointed it out as she spoke and she now noticed that it was quite difficult to see that it was indeed a window from inside the dining room. There was a sill in front of it on which Bob or his wife had placed a pot of ferns and two china ornaments and unless one looked very closely, the window behind was not obvious.

The Marquis looked to where Shana was pointing and told her,

"We certainly do not want to be overheard. Where do you suggest we sit?"

Shana indicated a table by the large window which looked out over the village green. It was opposite the main door into the dining room.

Bob had closed it and she was quite certain he would not be listening to their conversation.

She sat down as did the Marquis.

"What has happened, my Lord?"

"So much," the Marquis said, "that I hardly know where to begin."

"You mean they *came* to the Hall on Saturday night?"

"They came, but despite all your warnings it was a disaster."

Shana stared at him.

"How could it have been? What happened?"

"I took Dawkins into my confidence," the Marquis told her, "and we knew it would be impossible for him to tell the footmen that he knew one of them had been bribed to let in the burglars."

"I can quite understand that, my Lord, if you were not certain which one it was."

"I was suspicious of a young man I have employed for only a short time, but at the same time I could not ask any questions."

"No, or course not," Shana agreed.

"Dawkins and I", the Marquis continued, "therefore recruited three of the men from the stables who we were quite certain we could trust."

The Marquis paused and Shana realised that he was trying to explain to her every detail of what had occurred.

"We expected that they would enter the house, as you had heard the Italians say, by one of the windows, and we thought it would be one on the ground floor."

"And it was not?"

"The Italians had done their research well. There was a small amount of work being done at the far end of the West wing where one of the gutters was being replaced and the workmen had erected scaffolding."

Shana drew in her breath.

"So they came in through one of the upstairs windows."

"One on the first floor. It had never entered our heads that was what they might do."

"So what happened, my Lord?"

"We were waiting for them as soon as my guests had

retired to bed and my butler knew that the household had done the same."

Shana was listening intently and he went on,

"The footman they had bribed slept in the pantry and when he retired we knew who was intending to betray me and hand over the key of the safe."

"He had it in his possession?"

"Dawkins found it was missing from the place where he always kept it, but it was not taken until just before he would have gone to his bedroom."

Shana could see the plot was thickening and then she asked breathlessly,

"Do go on! What happened next?"

"We waited for perhaps a little over half-an-hour and then to our surprise instead of coming as we expected from a window on the ground floor, the two Italians came down the stairs which led directly to the kitchen quarters. They crept along the passage into the pantry and when we thought we had them cornered, we advanced in a body towards them."

"They were out-numbered," Shana said as if thinking to herself.

"At the first movement we made they were on the alert. They turned and one of them drew from his pocket what I thought was a bottle. Attached to it was a spray and he sprayed us in the face as we came through the door."

"A spray? But what was it, my Lord? What did it do?"

"It blinded us! And those who swallowed any of it started coughing uncontrollably."

Shana gave a deep sigh.

"So they escaped."

"They escaped, but as they passed the footman who

was waiting in the pantry to help them, they thrust a stiletto into him."

Shana let out a cry of horror.

"Is he dead?"

"Not dead but badly wounded. Then as they passed me, I managed, although I was coughing badly, to tear out of one of the Italian's hands a small case containing a plan of the house and some other papers."

"But they got away?"

"They got away," the Marquis repeated. "But I travelled to London first thing yesterday morning and visited the Italian Ambassador."

Shana stared at him in surprise.

"Why did you call on him?"

"Because this is a far more important incident that just two Italian rogues trying to steal my silver. In fact from what I learned from the Ambassador, you have, Miss Davis, stumbled onto something which is important internationally. Not only England and Italy are involved, but other countries as well."

For a moment Shana was silent before asking,

"I do not understand, my Lord. How could your burglary possibly be of international importance?"

The Marquis had been speaking in a low voice, but now he spoke even lower still as he replied,

"What I learned from the Ambassador was that for some time the authorities have been extremely worried concerning a gang of thieves who have concentrated on the most important treasures in every European country."

Shana gave a gasp, but she did not interrupt the Marquis.

"Top security agencies have been alerted in most European Capitals, but this was actually the first attempt, as far as they know, which has been made in England."

The Marquis glanced over his shoulder as if he was afraid someone was listening before he continued,

"Some very valuable pictures have been stolen in France, silver and irreplaceable porcelain in Germany, and it is the same story, I am told, in Spain."

"By these two Italians?" Shana asked. "I do not believe it."

"They are just part of a gang, and what is so serious is that it is thought that someone of standing, who has breeding and of course good taste, is at the head of it all."

Now Shana understood and she thought it was a very frightening scenario.

"Have they any idea," she asked, "of the nationality of the head man or where he lives?"

"They rather suspect he might be an Italian, but it could easily be someone in any of the other countries. All they know is that in a great number of cases, most of which have been hushed-up, priceless antiques have been stolen so cleverly and competently that no one has had the slightest idea until now what the thieves look like or indeed which country they come from."

"What a pity you did not catch them," Shana remarked.

There was a moment's silence and then the Marquis said,

"That, Miss Davis, is what *you* and I have to do."

Shana stared at him.

"I do not understand. What can – you do now that they have – gone?"

"They have indeed gone," the Marquis responded, "but *for the first time* someone concerned in a burglary has seen them, spoken to them and knows what they look like."

"Do you mean – *me*?"

"Exactly!" the Marquis exclaimed. "You are the one person, Miss Davis, who might be able to bring them to justice."

Shana made a gesture with her hands.

"I think that is impossible," she said. "Even if I described them to you, I doubt if it would be accurate enough to identify them and they have not actually taken anything which belongs to you."

"They attempted to do so and half-killed a man in the process," the Marquis responded quietly. "He may live but he is very badly hurt. That, as you well know, is a criminal offence for which his attackers should be arrested and brought to trial."

There was silence and then Shana said,

"I suppose so. But I expect by this time they have gone back to Italy."

"That is what the Ambassador thinks. So you will understand that we have to follow them."

Shana was very still.

"Did you say '*we*'?"

"I told the Ambassador exactly what had happened and he asked me to beg you to help in every way you can. Apparently in Italy they have already lost a great many national treasures from private houses and from museums. The same applies in France and Germany."

The Marquis became more positive as he continued,

"We have never, until this moment, had anything to go on. These thieves are so clever that they have made it impossible for them to be identified. In fact I forgot to tell you that they both wore masks on Saturday night."

"Masks!" Shana exclaimed.

"Although one was taller than the other," the Marquis

said. "I could never recognise either of them or be able to describe anything unusual about them."

"I am sure I can say the same," Shana came in quickly.

The Marquis shook his head.

"That is not true, Miss Davis, and you know it. You saw the men, you talked to them and as I already know you are very intelligent, I am sure, if you think carefully, you would know them if you met them again."

"I might do, but then it is very unlikely – I should meet them – again."

The Marquis bent forward.

"Now listen to me, Miss Davis. You have the chance of helping not only our own country but almost every other country in Europe. You are in a unique position which no man or woman has been in before. Is it really possible that you can say no?"

"I do not know – exactly what you are – asking me to do," Shana replied weakly.

"What I have arranged with the Ambassador, if you will agree, is that you and I will leave for Italy as swiftly as possible. *Tomorrow* if you can manage it."

Shana made a little sound of horror, but he continued,

"In Italy we will see a number of people who will tell us a lot about this gang which not even their Ambassador knows. He thinks that there is some place in Rome where they meet."

'But how could we find it?' Shana wanted to say but she could not stop the Marquis.

"The Italians suspect that the top man is an aristocrat," he announced. "In which case I might be able to meet him. If you are with me, through him we might come into contact with the two men you have already seen."

"You are being very plausible," Shana managed to

remark. "But you know, my Lord, you must be aware that this is just wishful thinking. It is only a million to one chance that I should ever get near those two thieves again."

She made a gesture with her hands before she added,

"If they are sensible they will disappear and if you are honest the only thing you have which is unusual about them is what you found in their case."

"I have not yet told you what was in the case. There were plans of houses and museums containing national treasures throughout England which would mean utter catastrophe if they were stolen."

"And you really think *I* can prevent it?" Shana asked. "You cannot be serious."

"I am *very* serious," the Marquis answered. "I can only plead with you to be patriotic and realise that as English citizens we cannot, either of us, refuse to help the Italians."

"But I – cannot go with you. It is – impossible."

"Why?" the Marquis asked. "Let me speak to your parents and I am sure they will agree that it is your duty, a desperate request which you cannot refuse."

When he mentioned her parents, Shana thought of her father.

If he had been there she knew he would have been only too willing to take her himself as he had solved so many problems for so many countries.

She recognised, because he had told her so much about intrigues and crimes which had taken place, but had been hushed up as it would be too upsetting and dangerous for the population as a rule to be aware of what had occurred.

'Papa would go,' she thought, 'and of course I would love to go with him.'

There was, however, no chance of her father returning to England for at least two or three weeks.

He had quite enough difficulties to solve wherever he was without having any more thrust upon him.

Almost as if he guessed what she was thinking, the Marquis said,

"I cannot believe that your father is not a very intelligent man. Therefore let me talk to him."

Shana drew in her breath.

"He is abroad, so we cannot consult him at the moment."

"And your mother?"

"My mother is dead."

"If I promise to look after you, protect you and make certain you will come to no harm, will you trust me?"

Shana did not answer and the Marquis went on,

"As the Ambassador has just said, if we can help to capture this gang we shall have the eternal gratitude of all the major countries in Europe. Not forgetting our own of course."

"You are very persuasive. But I don't know what to say."

"Then trust me," the Marquis entreated her. "As you can understand, it is very important that no one should know where we are going or why. When we arrive in Rome we will just be ordinary tourists until we have seen the Chief of Police and everyone else concerned with tracking down these clever, and until you unmask them, unidentified thieves."

The way he spoke was so impressive that Shana could not think of an answer.

"So that is settled," the Marquis exclaimed. "And I cannot believe you will let me down."

"I have not really – agreed," Shana protested.

The Marquis smiled.

"You know it is something you have to do just as if you were a soldier who has to obey his call to duty."

Shana thought he was talking like a General before a major battle.

"We have no choice," he continued, "but to agree that this is a demand of principle and patriotism."

Shana felt as if she was being swept off her feet, but equally she could not think of any good reason why she should refuse to help the Italians.

She knew how much they valued all the treasures which had accumulated in their highly artistic country over the centuries. She and her father had discussed this subject so often and the same applied to all the other countries the Marquis had mentioned.

The French had suffered from losing so many great works of art and furniture during the Revolution and they would certainly have no wish to lose any more.

The Germans had always been avaricious and they wanted to possess more treasures in Berlin than other countries possessed in their Capital cities.

She knew how much her father appreciated the works of art his family had collected and at the same time he talked proudly about treasures in the British Museum and the National Gallery almost as if he owned them himself.

Shana next quizzed the Marquis,

"When they steal these treasures what do the thieves do with them?"

"No one knows exactly where they go to, but the Ambassador told me they suspect that one man may be making a huge collection for himself. A number of treasures are certainly going to America because they have the money to pay for them."

Shana stared at him.

"America!" she exclaimed. "I never thought of that."

"It may be just an idea, but at the same time as they are exploring Europe, they are openly buying pictures from our ancestral homes."

The Marquis rose to his feet.

"I expect, Miss Davis, you will want to pack some clothes. I will pick you up here early tomorrow morning, unless you wish me to collect you elsewhere."

It was impossible, Shana thought, to go on arguing with him.

For a moment she felt angry as he was pushing her into doing something which was intimidating and frightening.

He had already made it impossible for her to refuse him outright and she wanted to have time to think. Perhaps even to find a way she could identify the men without having to travel to Italy.

Once again the Marquis read her thoughts.

"There is no way out. And perhaps it will not be as unpleasant as it appears at this moment."

He twisted his lips as he spoke and he was thinking there was no other woman of his acquaintance who would refuse to go with him anywhere he might suggest.

Shana did not reply.

"My yacht, at the moment, is moored in the Thames just below the House of Commons. I have already sent a messenger to tell them that we will be coming aboard tomorrow morning."

"You have – already done that?" Shana asked in astonishment. "How could you know that I would agree to do what you are demanding?"

"I could not believe that you would refuse," the Marquis replied. "I have realised you are most intelligent and I was convinced that you would understand how important our mission is. It would be impossible for us as British citizens to refuse such a cry for help."

He saw Shana's eyes flicker and continued,

"The Ambassador has told me they are desperate and this is the first ray of hope they have had in two years."

"Two years!" Shana cried. "Is that how long this thieving has been taking place?"

"They did not realise at first that it was the same people. Now they are convinced that thefts carried out in the Royal Palace in Vienna two years ago, when the criminals carried away some of the Crown Jewels and a dozen irreplaceable pictures, are connected with important thefts in other Capital cities."

"How can they be sure?"

"Because they always work in the same way and take only valuables of the sixteenth and seventeenth centuries."

"They might have taken more from you than they had intended."

"I can assure you that if they had succeeded, which they would have done without your warning, they would have been very proud to possess what was in my safe. The jewellery alone, which is seldom worn, is worth nearly a hundred thousand pounds."

Shana's eyes widened.

"Then surely it was very casual of you not to keep it in a safer place."

"I had always imagined that my own home was safe and the staff in it were faithful to me."

His voice was sharp as he added,

"I shall not make the same mistake again. Most of the silver and jewellery in the safe has now been moved to my bank in London.

"That is most wise of you," Shana remarked.

"If it had not been for you, Miss Davis, I might have been devastated by losing it all. Quite frankly, I want to save other people from losing what they value most in the world."

Again Shana realised she could not argue with him.

"What – time," she asked in a small voice, "shall I be here waiting – for you tomorrow morning?"

The Marquis's eyes lit up.

"So you are *really* coming?"

"You leave me with no alternative. I think it is – something I should not do and I hope no one will ever know – where I have gone."

"I will make quite sure that our journey is completely secret. If I pick you up here, my servants at the Hall will not know you are travelling with me. I thought we would tell Bob Grimes that, as I am driving to London tomorrow morning, I have offered you a lift as you are going to stay with friends."

Shana nodded.

"I am sure he will believe it."

The Marquis held out his hand.

"Thank you, Miss Davis, for trusting me and for being very patriotic. We must not forget those criminals left behind them a man they thought was dead."

Shana shuddered.

"If he recovers, he may be able to tell us a little about them. But I doubt if he knows much more than we know ourselves."

"I have a horrible feeling," Shana told him, "that they may have intended to kill him – anyway before removing their – spoils."

"I thought that too and from what I have heard they are completely merciless and usually leave a number of dead bodies behind after they have taken what they want."

"In that case," Shana murmured, "I hope we survive."

"I hope so too," the Marquis said. "And I promise that whatever happens, I will not allow you to go into any danger."

"I doubt if you could really prevent it, but of course I would like you to try."

She looked up at him as she spoke and when their eyes met she knew they were appraising her.

She had the feeling that he was finding her very different from what he had expected and he was trying to puzzle out what she was really like.

Shana turned towards the door.

"I must go and see Mrs. Grimes before I leave and make some excuse for having to go to London in such a hurry."

"I am sure you have friends there."

"Not many. Actually I much prefer being in the country."

"Then let us hope that our journey will not take too long and we shall be successful quicker than we expect."

"You are just saying that to make me less nervous than I am already," Shana pointed out. "And I think it will be a miracle if it turns out as you hope it will."

"Believe it or not," the Marquis replied, "miracles do happen and the first has occurred already."

She looked at him in surprise uncertain what he meant.

"Have you forgotten that you are the only person in the world who has actually seen the criminals we are pursuing? Europe has been looking for them for two years."

"Then all I can say is that Europe is either very unlucky or very inefficient!"

She walked from the room as she spoke and as she turned towards the stairs she heard the Marquis laugh.

She did not realise he was thinking that Miss Davis was the most unusual woman he had ever encountered.

Not only because she had no wish to be with him, which he had never experienced before, but also because she seldom said what he expected her to say.

He was not so stupid that he did not realise she could never be what she was pretending to be. No one could look less like a cook at a village inn.

She spoke like a lady and was proficient in several languages.

She had said that she was a teacher and he could not imagine what sort of school in the country she would be teaching in, as she would be wasting her time if she was teaching the alphabet to village children.

Was there something very wrong with her outlook on life or her family background?

He was extremely curious and if nothing else, she would give him plenty to think about on the voyage to Rome.

As far as he was concerned this expedition had come at exactly the right moment as he needed to escape from Lady Irene and what could be better than for him to disappear abroad where she could not follow him?

Most of his guests on Monday morning had driven back to London in their own carriages.

When he told Lady Irene that he had arranged an important meeting in London very early, she had insisted that he must change it.

"We will get to London in time for luncheon, dearest," she had said. "We can eat in my house and there will be no reason for you to hurry away when it is finished."

The Marquis knew exactly what she meant and had no intention of agreeing to her invitation.

He had decided after the drama on Saturday night that

it would be impossible for him ever again to visit Irene's bedroom.

In fact he had no desire to do so. Quite suddenly, as it had happened to him before in his life, his interest in her had vanished.

She no longer attracted him and he could not explain to himself or anyone else why this change had occurred unexpectedly.

For the Marquis there should always be a quick ending to a love affair.

But he had, where Irene was concerned, no wish for a scene as he recognised only too well the tears and accusations there would be if he told her the truth,

He therefore made the excuse on Sunday night that he had contracted a bad headache and was retiring to bed early.

On Monday morning he left her a note and when she was called it was handed to her by her lady's maid.

"His Lordship says as your Ladyship was to have this letter as soon as you woke," she said.

Lady Irene had sat up in bed and there was a hard expression in her eyes as she opened the envelope.

The Marquis wrote that he was deeply distressed at not being able to escort her to London. He had an urgent message from the Prime Minister and he had to be at 10 Downing Street by half-past ten.

He followed this information with a polished compliment about her looks and how delightful it had been to welcome her as a guest at the Hall, but he made no reference to calling later in the day at her house.

Lady Irene's lips were set in a hard line as she descended the stairs later in the morning.

She drove to London with her lady's maid in her comfortable carriage.

The Marquis had no intention of letting her know that he was going abroad and it would be a mistake for her to talk about his arrangements. It was therefore wiser to leave her guessing for the rest of the week whether he was in the country or London.

When she finally realised the truth that their affair had ended, there was nothing she would be able to do about it.

The Marquis knew she might want to continue her pursuit of him, but by that time he would be in the Mediterranean.

He had a great many matters to see to at the Hall before he left and there were innumerable instructions for his secretary.

"I am surprised at your going away, my Lord, just as the shooting season has started," the secretary commented.

"I do not suppose I shall be very long," the Marquis explained. "But it is something I have to do and I am not able to refuse."

His secretary guessed that his travels were something to do with the Prince of Wales or perhaps with the Prime Minister with whom he knew his Lordship was very friendly.

"Just keep things going," the Marquis ordered, "until I return. I do not expect to be away for any length of time."

"Your Lordship can leave everything to me," his secretary assured him.

"I know," the Marquis replied. "You are always very tactful."

His secretary laughed.

"I want to believe that, my Lord. And if you need a rest from those who talk too much and never leave your Lordship alone, who could blame you?"

"Who indeed? And I think I am entitled to a short holiday."

He did not say any more and his secretary wondered what he was up to now.

If it was a woman, he had no idea who she was. He knew even better than the Marquis himself that Lady Irene was on her way out.

'A good job too,' he thought. 'I never did like that woman. She may be beautiful, but she had nothing else to offer.'

CHAPTER FOUR

Shana and Betty, her maid, packed a large trunk with her clothes and hats.

"It looks as if you be going away for a long time, miss," Betty commented.

"I don't think it will be very long, but I do not know exactly what we will be doing, so I must take a variety of clothes."

Betty seemed satisfied with Shana's explanation and did not ask her any more questions.

When she finally retired to bed she turned over and over in her mind what she was pushed into and could only come to the conclusion that, although she must go to Rome with the Marquis, her father would not approve.

'I can hardly ask the Marquis to take a chaperone with us,' she thought.

Then she told herself she was being very stupid. As he was known as being so fastidious and particular with whom he associated, he was not likely to be interested in a girl who was alternatively a teacher and a cook.

Another problem was of course getting to the *Rose and Crown* in the morning.

Baker she knew would be the most curious of the servants and she had told him that she wanted to spend a little time with Mrs. Grimes before leaving to stay with friends. She had therefore arranged to be picked up from the *Rose and Crown*.

Baker accepted this without comment and Shana told him,

"I have asked Mrs. Baker to be very kind and send Mrs. Grimes some food every day. There is no one at the *Rose and Crown* who can cook and she must keep up her strength."

"I'll see to it, Miss Shana," Baker said stiffly. "And I suppose one of the grooms can take it to her."

"Yes, of course," Shana agreed.

She thought she must remember to tell Bob that the food was coming daily for his wife and to be careful not to say she would be driving off with the Marquis.

'Being in disguise,' she thought to herself, 'is horribly difficult. I hope it is something I do not have to do again. Once is quite enough!'

It was not merely a question of once.

Shana was feeling very nervous about what would happen when they reached Rome and she considered that the Marquis and the Italian Ambassador had made much too much out of her contact and sight of the Italians.

The Officials in Rome who were really concerned with catching the thieves would think her contribution of little importance.

'Anyway, if they are not impressed, I shall be able to come home all the quicker,' she decided.

Then she remembered that she would have to persuade the Marquis to bring her back for it would be impossible for her to return alone.

She tried not to think of everything that might go wrong, but endless snags kept jumping up in front of her and she could not escape from them.

*

The groom brought the chaise round at half-past nine and it did not take them long to reach the *Rose and Crown.*

As soon as the groom had unloaded her luggage in the stable yard, Shana sent him back as it would be a mistake for him to see the Marquis arrive. He would be bound to tell Baker his Lordship had been at the *Rose and Crown* at the same time as her.

She ran upstairs to see Mrs. Grimes, who was better, but still in pain.

"I 'ears you's goin' away, Miss Shana," she said. "I don't know what we'll do without you, you've been so kind to us and we'll never forget your 'elp."

"I have told the staff at home to bring you some food every day and I am sure there will be enough for your husband too."

Mrs. Grimes clasped her hands together.

"You're an angel! And I'll say a prayer for you every night. You're that pretty it's time you 'ad an 'usband."

Shana laughed.

"There is no hurry for *that* and you know we are rather short of tall, handsome Don Juans in Hertfordshire."

She did not expect Mrs. Grimes to know who Don Juan was, but she understood the gist of what she was saying.

"One'll turn up sooner or later," Mrs. Grimes remarked. "You mark me words."

"I do hope so you are right," Shana laughed.

She thought she heard the sound of wheels and said goodbye to Mrs. Grimes.

She came downstairs to find that she was right.

The Marquis had arrived a little earlier than expected and Shana was thankful she had sent her own chaise back home quickly.

73

She just had time to say to Bob Grimes,

"Be careful not to let his Lordship know who I am and no one must know who is driving me to London."

Bob nodded as the Marquis came in through the back door.

He was so tall he seemed to fill the whole narrow passage and he looked pleased when he saw Shana.

He did not say anything, but his groom, without being told, picked up Shana's luggage and pilled it into the Marquis's impressive fourgon which was drawn by four perfectly matched stallions.

Shana thought no one could possess a better conveyance, even if travelling towards disaster.

The Marquis was obviously in a hurry. Having said farewell to Bob he stepped into the driving seat.

Only as they moved out of the yard and onto the road did he say to Shana,

"You are punctual, which is unusual in a woman. Or were you anxious to get away so that no one will know where we are going?"

"I hope no one does know," Shana answered. "Although I do not think anyone would believe it."

The Marquis smiled.

"I agree that it does all sound rather far-fetched. But we now have something positive to convince us. The wretched footman the Italian stabbed died this morning!"

"Oh, I am sorry!" Shana exclaimed.

She thought it was a miserable way for a young man to lose his life.

As the Marquis did not say any more, they drove on in silence.

She saw at once that he was as expert with the reins

like her father and she had to admit she had never driven behind a finer team of horses.

They were travelling too fast for there to be much conversation on the journey between her and the Marquis.

When they neared the outskirts of London, she was certain he must have broken every record, but he had to drive more slowly through the traffic.

Next they reached the Thames and when Shana saw the Marquis's yacht moored off the Embankment, she was most impressed. It was far larger and more graceful than she had expected.

"I have only had the *Seashell* for two years," the Marquis explained as they drove up alongside her. "I hope you enjoy every innovation I have installed including electric light."

Shana's eyes widened in surprise.

Her father had told her that a few years earlier electric light had been installed in the Transatlantic steamers going to America, but she had not expected smaller vessels to follow suit so quickly.

She was to find however that the *Seashell* was equipped with every new invention that had ever been thought of and at the same time it was extremely prettily decorated.

As she walked into the Saloon, she could not help exclaiming with delight.

"I am glad you like my yacht," the Marquis said. "I designed it myself. I see no reason because one is at sea that one should not please the eye as well as the body."

"It is very pretty!" Shana exclaimed.

There were masses of flowers arranged in vases in the Saloon and she wondered if the Marquis always provided flowers on his yacht or if they had been ordered because he was bringing a lady on board.

Then she told herself she was being very naïve.

Of course the Marquis did not travel alone and Shana suspected that he was accompanied by a female companion on every voyage he undertook.

As soon as they came aboard, the Marquis ordered the Captain to put to sea.

They were, in fact, moving down the river before the team that had brought them from the country was turning away from the Embankment.

Luncheon was ready, but the Marquis suggested that Shana might like to see her cabin before they ate and she was taken below by the Steward.

The cabin was as attractive as the Saloon. A pink chintz covered the portholes with the same material on the bed. It was echoed in the silk curtains which fell from a gold corolla fastened to the ceiling.

There were flowers on the dressing table and a thick carpet on the floor.

Shana thought it would be impossible for any vessel to be more attractively decorated.

She had travelled to the Mediterranean with her father when he had taken her to Venice and her cabin, she thought, had been rather drab and dull in comparison.

She was fascinated to find that there was a bathroom leading off her cabin, so she washed her hands and after she had taken off her hat, she went above.

By this time they were moving very fast down river and it occurred to Shana that the Marquis was in just as much hurry to reach Rome and complete their mission as she was.

When she found him in the Saloon, he seemed relaxed and at his ease.

"I thought as it is the beginning of our adventure," he said, "that we should drink our own health in champagne.

You certainly deserve a glass."

"For what particular reason?" Shana enquired.

"Because unlike most women you did not want to talk when we were driving," he replied, "so I could concentrate on my horses."

She thought he was being somewhat provocative and therefore replied,

"Which of course are more important than women at any time!"

"I would not be so impolite as to make such a suggestion," the Marquis retorted. "But there is a time and a place for everything and I find most women talk too much."

"To be quite frank," Shana said, "you are warning me that the less I say the more you will appreciate my company."

"You are twisting what I am saying and actually I was trying to pay you a compliment."

"Which of course I must be very grateful for, considering they are often in short supply," Shana countered.

The Marquis reflected that this was a very different conversation from his usual exchanges with most women, who would be flattering him whilst making it clear that they wanted to talk about themselves.

He found everything he said at luncheon was answered in a different way from his expectations and then when she had just made him laugh, Shana was suddenly serious.

"I have just thought of something," she muttered.

"What is it?"

"We are going to Rome, but I do not have a passport."

The Marquis smiled.

"Now you are underestimating my powers of organisation."

"You mean you have brought one for me?"

Shana was thinking that when she had travelled abroad her name had been attached to her father's passport in the form of a letter signed by the Secretary of State for Foreign Affairs.

She could hardly have produced it, or one of her own, even if she had one and, in fact of course, her father had taken his passport with him when he left England.

"When the Italian Ambassador," the Marquis was saying, "told me it was imperative that you and I should go to Italy immediately, I remembered that you would need a passport, but he thought as the cook at the *Rose and Crown* you would probably not have one."

"So what did you do?"

"I have had you added to my own passport," the Marquis replied.

"How could you do that?"

"I thought that if we were to arrive in Rome and mix with a variety of people ranging from those of social position to those who might be suspected of being burglars, it was important there should not be any questions asked as to why you were accompanying me."

Shana knew this to be true, but she could not think what he could do about it.

"If I was to arrive in Rome using my own name," the Marquis added, "it would be impossible to say you were my wife when we meet people who would know I am not married."

"Of course you could not do that," Shana said quickly.

"Also a number of Italians who visit England every year know I do not have a sister," the Marquis continued. "But, as it happens, I have a cousin who is a Brooke although she is somewhat younger than you."

"How old is she?"

"She is seventeen, but I think it unlikely that any Italian has ever heard of her. Her parents live in Yorkshire and seldom come to London."

"So you have attached her name to your passport?"

"I might have made it difficult for you by using my cousin's Christian name, but fortunately when I was having luncheon that first day with my friends who were shooting with me, I heard Bob call you 'Miss Shana'."

Shana drew in her breath. She had no idea that the Marquis had heard Bob speaking to her at the *Rose and Crown*. He might have said something else to make the Marquis suspicious that she was not who she pretended to be.

"I thought it a rather unusual, but charming name, so when I asked the Ambassador if I could have your name added to my passport, I put you down as 'Miss Shana Brooke'. By a happy coincidence my cousin's name is Sarah, so the two names have a likeness to each other."

"Yes, indeed," Shana replied. "I think it was clever of you to make me your cousin."

"It will save your reputation and mine," the Marquis smiled. "And may I say my cousin is a very attractive young woman, but not as beautiful as you."

"Thank you, my Lord, I will do my best to play the part convincingly."

"I am sure you will and let me say I can imagine no one who could do it better."

She thought he was being complimentary because he had been afraid she would resent being added to his passport under another name, but she had to admit it was very astute of him as she had completely forgotten about her passport in the hurry and flurry of setting off on the journey.

When luncheon was over the Marquis went on the bridge to watch the yacht moving into the open sea.

Shana descended to her own cabin.

She found the Marquis's valet, Curtis, had unpacked her clothes and had taken away her trunk and hatbox.

He was a dapper little man and she thanked him.

"I'll do my best to look after you, miss," he said, "and I only hopes you're not going to be seasick."

"You need not worry about me," Shana told him. "I am a good sailor and the last time I was at sea we ran into a very bad storm and I was the only woman who was not prostrate in her cabin."

"That's just what I likes to hear and if there's anything you may want, miss, you asks me and I'll get it for you."

"I think this yacht is the smartest and certainly the most beautiful I have ever seen," Shana sighed.

"Have you seen the library?" Curtis asked.

"Library?"

He pointed to a cabin across the corridor.

"This be his Lordship's special introduction," he said as he opened the door. "He can't stand a long voyage without having something to read."

Shana followed him and gasped.

The Marquis had turned a large cabin into a sitting room with a desk rather like the one she had seen in his study at the Hall.

The walls of the cabin were covered with books from the floor to the ceiling and there were two portholes, but otherwise there were just books and more books.

Shana clapped her hands.

"I have never seen anything so wonderful," she cried. "I am sure no other yacht can boast a cabin like this. I hope

I may borrow one or two of these fabulous volumes."

"I'll fetch you anything you wants," Curtis told her. "You'll find, as his Lordship does, them books be often more interesting than them as talks their heads off in the Saloon!"

Shana laughed.

"I can understand that and please may I take two books now into my cabin so that I will have something to read when I retire to bed?"

"Help yourself, miss. There's enough for you and his Lordship without leaving no gaps on the shelves."

He left the cabin and Shana looked through the books with interest.

Some of them she had already read and there were others she immediately wanted to read and thought they would have interested her father as a great number were in different European languages.

She found a book on Rome which she thought he would find interesting.

Then as if drawn automatically, she found a great number of books on Greece and many in Greek. She took three of these, hoping that Curtis would not think she was being greedy and carried them to her cabin.

This library was something she had not expected to find at sea.

She had put two or three books of her own in her luggage as she too hated to be without something to read.

She went up on deck and was standing looking at the coast of England as the yacht moved further out to sea.

The Marquis joined her.

"I am sorry if I seem to be neglecting you," he began, "but I always enjoy the moment when the *Seashell* is out on the waves. I do not know whether you have noticed, but we are going at what the Captain claims is a record speed for a yacht of this size."

"I thought it was moving very fast," Shana admitted, "and of course it is important for us to reach Italy as soon as possible. We can then be back before anyone begins to wonder what has happened to us."

"Will there be many people worrying about you with the exception of Bob?" the Marquis enquired. "I think you said your father is abroad."

"He is and I am hoping I will be back before he returns."

"Then we must do our best not to worry him."

There was a little pause before the Marquis asked,

"What does your father do?"

Shana thought quickly how she should reply.

"I have always been told that if you are playing a part and in disguise it is important not only what you say but what you think. I am trying to think myself into the part of being your cousin."

"In other words you do not want to talk about yourself. I have never met a woman who does not want to tell me the story of her life."

"Mine is not at all exciting and I therefore have no wish to talk about it," Shana said firmly.

The Marquis did not speak and she continued,

"What I would really enjoy would be an extensive tour of the *Seashell*. Could I please see the engines and of course the whole layout of the yacht itself?"

The Marquis looked at her in surprise.

"Do you really mean that?"

"You asked me what I would like to do."

"Very well, but you must tell me if you find it bores

you. I find it absorbing, but that is because I have planned so much of it myself."

As they walked round the yacht the Marquis found that Shana asked extremely intelligent questions and she was also charming to the seamen.

Finally they finished up in the galley with the Chef. Having enjoyed an excellent luncheon, she was not surprised to find that he was a Frenchman.

She spoke to him in French and he was delighted to tell her about some new recipes which he had yet not prepared for his Lordship. He told her he would be cooking two of them for dinner tonight.

"They sound delightful," Shana enthused. "It is something I shall look forward to."

The Marquis was aware that she spoke perfect Parisian French and it only added to the curiosity he felt about her.

When they went below to change for dinner, she told him his valet had shown her the library.

"I am thrilled with your books," she said fervently.

The Marquis thought with a feeling of relief she was so unlike Lady Irene or other women he had brought on the yacht and she would not expect him to be continually at her side, talking to her about herself.

When they sat down to dinner he asked her which books she had chosen and she told him the title of the one on Rome and mentioned the three Greek books.

"Why are you so interested in Greece?" he asked.

"It is a place I want to visit more than anywhere else in the world and I was thrilled to find some books of yours on Greece which I have not read."

"I suppose you realise that two of them are in Greek."

"Yes, I know."

"Are you telling me," the Marquis quizzed her

incredulously, "that you speak Greek?"

"Of course I do. Why not?"

"There is no 'of course' about it. Greek is one of the most important languages in Europe, as I have found myself. How is it possible, looking as young as you do, that you can speak so many languages?"

"I have spoken them ever since I was a child," Shana answered. "And I had a very good teacher."

"I thought that was what you were."

"It is what I would like to be, but when I think about Greece I am always conscious of how fortunate we were in having such brilliant and intelligent people to guide us."

She thought the Marquis looked slightly disdainful as she continued,

"After all we owe to the Greeks the beginning of sciences and indeed the beginning of thought."

"Now why should you say that?"

"If you have read the history of Greece and the books written by the Greeks, you should not ask that question."

Because the Marquis enjoyed an argument he replied,

"Plato said that the Egyptians looked upon the Greeks as children. Too young and too innocent to be the creators of anything."

"The Egyptians," Shana said scornfully, "worshipped Gods who were so old they were crumbling away. The Greeks with the freshness of youth sought out new Gods which they shaped in their own image."

She paused and as the Marquis did not say anything she went on,

"Who could be more wonderful than Apollo, the God of Light, and Athene, the Patron Goddess of Athens, the centre of Greek civilisation?"

She spoke passionately and quite unexpectedly the

Marquis laughed.

"I do not believe it," he exclaimed. "Who are you and where have you come from, unless it is Mount Olympus?"

Because she could not help it, Shana laughed too and then they started arguing again.

By the time the yacht had passed through the Bay of Biscay, Shana thought they had argued about almost everything she could ever imagine.

They discussed the countries of Europe one by one and she always attacked anything the Marquis stated as fact as it was more amusing than agreeing with everything he said.

She queried his conclusions, whatever they might be.

He enjoyed their sparring with words as much as she did and he conceded, although it annoyed him to do so, that she was sometimes better informed on a particular subject than he was.

'She is not real,' he told himself again when they retired to bed.

They were later than they had meant to be simply because they were absorbed in duelling with each other.

He had expected Shana to be bright, enthusiastic and of course submissive to anything he suggested, but he found that he had to polish up his brain to compete with her.

Although it seemed impossible, she often knew more than he did about a country they were discussing, but he had no idea that it was because her father had spent so much time in Europe, who as Secretary of State for Foreign Affairs, was conversant with national problems which were not known to very many people.

Shana was a walking encyclopaedia of almost everything about the places they talked about, so that when they reached the Mediterranean the Marquis had to admit he had never enjoyed a voyage more.

He had not expected, however, to have to exert himself so strongly to prevent being mentally overpowered. Not by a philosopher but a beautiful and exceptionally clever young woman.

When they put in to Gibraltar to refuel the Marquis said to Shana,

"Now we will go ashore and you must allow me to buy you a present. The shops in Gibraltar are famous and I am sure we shall find something you will really like."

"That would be wonderful!" Shana replied. "What I would love is a book on Gibraltar because, believe it or not, there isn't one in your library."

"There must be."

"Then *you* find it," Shana retorted. "I looked last night because I thought it would be interesting for us to talk about its strange history, but I could not find one."

"Then we will certainly buy one. But I am sure you would really like something more personal."

"Nothing could be more personal than a book which will go into my brain and stay there forever. I am sure you know that everything we put into our brain remains there and however hard we try we cannot remove it."

The Marquis had not thought about this before.

"I wonder if that is a psychological fact," he quizzed, "or just part of your imagination?"

"It *is* a psychological fact. I was reading a book the other day by an extremely well-known scientist who said how important it was that we appreciate this point when we are dealing with children."

She paused and then added slowly,

"And of course feeding our own minds with what makes us happy and not with what can distress or trouble us."

The Marquis tried to query her statement, but he knew at the end it was another battle that Shana had won.

What astonished him when they reached Gibraltar was that she was not interested in the kind of present he was anxious to give her. He had never been there before without the woman who was accompanying him demanding jewellery.

The coral in Gibraltar was famous and they would beg him to give it to them combined if possible with diamonds.

Also they would not have thought of leaving the port without several of the exquisitely embroidered Chinese shawls which hung from the ceiling in almost every shop.

He had difficulty in persuading Shana to accept one of these which he thought would enhance her beauty and she refused to even enter the jewellery shops, saying positively that she did not want anything they sold.

Then the Marquis asked why and to his surprise she blushed.

"Tell me," he said. "I want to give you something which will make you remember this trip."

"I can remember it without a present, although thank you very much for thinking of it."

The Marquis was silent for a moment and then he remarked,

"I have the feeling, or shall I say I am reading your thoughts, that you consider it incorrect to accept anything expensive from a man."

She looked away and he realised that what he had said was true.

"I know exactly what your mother said to you, that you may accept gloves, scent or flowers but nothing else."

"I can accept books."

"Which I have already bought for you and while I

understand your reasons for refusing, I would like to give you, as my cousin, a coral necklace and perhaps ear-rings to go with it."

He spoke so persuasively that Shana eventually capitulated.

"Very well," she said. "But it must not be expensive – just pretty."

The Marquis was not only bemused but bewildered.

'Why does this young woman behave as if she was a *debutante* of some important social Dowager' he asked himself.

She was a lady. He had known it from the first time he had spoken to her, but her parents must be poor if she was forced to earn her own living, so in which case it seemed absurd for her to keep to the social rules intended for those who thought of themselves as upper class.

'I do not understand,' the Marquis muttered to himself.

When they sat down to dinner that night, Shana was wearing the coral necklace and matching ear-rings, which she had finally been persuaded to accept as his gift.

She looked very lovely, sitting opposite him at the dinner table wearing a white evening gown and as if to celebrate the occasion she had fastened one pink rose in her hair.

It passed through the Marquis's mind that if the Prince of Wales could see her now he would pursue her relentlessly.

It was therefore important that they never met.

The Marquis could think of quite a number of men who would also be dangerous if he introduced them to Shana, and he considered it would be not only a pity but wrong for him to do so.

'She is unspoilt and very innocent,' he told himself. 'She has no idea how dangerous the outside world could be to her.'

He wondered what would happen to her in the future when they returned to England and supposed it was doubtful he would ever see her again.

Perhaps she would marry some young man in the country and they would have a large family.

'Yet,' he meditated, 'where would there be a man who was clever and intelligent enough to keep her interested? And to understand her strange and almost bewildering brain that makes her different in every way from any other woman, especially Lady Irene.'

He continued to argue with himself.

'Even if she has been trained to be a teacher, how is it possible she can be so original and so extraordinarily well-read at her age?'

His mind continued to ponder.

'The very most she can be is twenty-two or twenty-three and she looks very much younger – why?'

Finally he admitted he could not make any sense of her at all and yet he intended to unravel the mystery of Shana from the *Rose and Crown* before their mission came to an end.

*

Shana had enjoyed exploring Gibraltar and had expected they would leave the next morning.

However the Captain of the *Seashell* was concerned with the ship's oil tanks overheating and the Chef was having difficulty finding the right ingredients he required for his new recipes.

The Marquis therefore agreed somewhat reluctantly that they would stay for another day.

To Shana's delight he hired a carriage and they drove across the frontier into Spain, but there was not a great deal to see.

The Marquis noted her interest in everything wherever they went, as they discussed recent elements of history of Spain and the new Spanish artists and musicians who had become famous throughout Europe.

"I have enjoyed myself *so* much," Shana enthused when they returned to the yacht. "Thank you a thousand times for taking me. You are so kind."

"I really enjoyed myself too," the Marquis said and knew he was speaking the truth.

They changed for dinner and because it was a warm night they went up on deck afterwards to see the lights of Gibraltar.

They could see the ships steaming into and out of port while the moon overhead and the stars glittering in the sky made the world enchanting.

"Why must we travel on to make ourselves unhappy with all we will be facing in Rome? It is so beautiful here I cannot bear to leave it," Shana sighed.

She was speaking more to herself than to the Marquis.

"You are quite right," he responded. "You should never be surrounded by anything but beauty, and that is what I would like to give you."

"The sea," she said dreamily, "the stars in the sky and the moon and of course the flowers. Who could ask for anything more?"

Quite suddenly the Marquis knew that he wanted more.

A great deal more.

Yet he realised it would be a mistake to put his feelings into words.

Even more of a mistake to break the very comfortable and enjoyable rapport there now existed between them.

When a little while later they left the deck, Shana said,

"I think I must retire to bed and thank you again for a wonderful day."

There was a softness and something almost mystical in her voice that the Marquis detected.

She did not wait for him to reply, but walked down the companionway and he heard the door of her cabin close.

It was when he strolled to his own cabin that he found himself thinking that he was behaving very differently from the way he had ever behaved in his life.

Never had he been alone with a woman for so long before she had surrendered herself into his arms. Throwing back her head she would wait impatiently for his kisses.

As he undressed he was thinking of Shana.

She never appeared, either by anything she said or by the expression in her eyes, to think of him as an attractive and desirable man.

He appreciated that she enjoyed talking with him and her eyes sparkled when they sparred with each other.

She would jump for joy when she scored a point at his expense, but it was all wholly impersonal.

He might have been her brother.

Because the situation was so new and something that had never happened to him before, he could hardly believe it was possible.

He was only too familiar with that certain look in a woman's eyes, the provocative pout to her lips and the way her hand touched him as if accidentally because she found him so irresistible.

They still would have a few days together before they reached Rome.

'What am I waiting for?' the Marquis demanded of himself.

They had already spent four days on board the

Seashell and none of his friends would believe that he had not yet attempted to kiss Shana.

The idea had entered his mind a thousand times, but he remembered he had promised to protect her and that meant not only from other men but from himself.

Yet was that what she really wanted?

He had thought that tonight when they were looking at the beauty of the sea and the stars, there had been a different note in her voice.

She had seemed as if she was afraid of losing such an enchanting world.

'It is all part of love,' he thought. 'And what young woman does not want love?'

He walked to the open porthole and looked out. The moonlight was gleaming on the sea and everything was very quiet.

'*What am I waiting for*?' the Marquis asked himself again.

He walked across the cabin which was the Master Suite and Shana's cabin was next to his.

He opened her door very quietly.

CHAPTER FIVE

The cabin was in darkness.

The Marquis stood still for a moment and then he reached out his hand and turned on the electric switch.

There were three lights in the cabin and he lit the one which was attached to the gold corolla over the bed. He chose this light because it was not as strong as the others and he thought more romantic.

Now he could see that Shana was asleep in the bed as he pulled the door to and walked towards her.

If it had been any other woman, her sleep would have been a pretence and when he reached the bed she would wake up with a start and appear surprised to see him.

Shana did not move and he realised that she was in fact fast asleep.

He stood looking down at her and thought no one could be lovelier.

Her eyelashes against her perfect skin were darker than her hair and the Marquis appreciated how long they were.

She was lying back against the pillows completely relaxed, her hands on the sheet in front of her and because it was a warm night, the sheet was low enough to reveal the outline of the curves of her figure beneath a diaphanous nightgown.

The Marquis looked down at her and Shana appeared to him even more desirable and beautiful.

He felt the blood throbbing in his temples and he knew that he had only to bend forward to hold her lips captive.

Then because she looked so young, so innocent and so helpless, he paused.

He had promised to protect her, but did she really want to be protected *from him*?

Was this another part of the act?

He felt that he had been very patient so far and no man in his position would have waited so long for the response which had never come.

'I want her,' he thought. 'I want her as I have never wanted a woman in my life.'

Yet something still stopped him – something which made him feel as if she was in some way protected.

Not only by her own innocence, but by some spiritual force in the form of a shield around her sleeping body.

He started to tell himself this was all nonsense. He was a man and she was a very lovely and desirable woman.

What else could be expected to happen when they were alone on his yacht?

'I want her! I want her!' he felt his body insisting, yet still he hesitated.

Then as if an angel, or whoever was protecting Shana, won the battle and he turned away.

He could not hurt or even touch anything so perfect, so beautiful and so pure.

He walked back to the door, turned out the light and returned to his own cabin.

Only when he was in bed, knowing it was going to be very hard for him to sleep, did he ask himself if he was a fool or a saint.

Quite unaware that the Marquis had visited her cabin the previous night, Shana woke early.

The sun was streaming through the porthole and when she looked out she thought the Mediterranean was as blue as the Madonna's robe.

The yacht was already moving out of port on the Marquis's orders and she wanted to say goodbye to Gibraltar and enjoy the view as they steamed along the coast of Spain.

When the Marquis came up for breakfast he saw her hanging over the rail, staring out at the Spanish coast.

"You are very early, Shana," he commented as he joined her.

"It is almost wicked to stay in bed on such a beautiful day," she replied. "And I am afraid of missing something."

"You will have plenty to admire in Rome."

"That is what I have been thinking and I want to see everything. The fountain of the Trevi and of course the Colosseum."

"I suppose," the Marquis said, "you are going to throw some coins into the Trevi and make a wish, as every tourist does."

"Of course they do and I am sure all their wishes come true."

"What will you wish for?" the Marquis asked as they were walking towards the Saloon and when he sat down at the breakfast table he finished his question with,

"A handsome lover or something that glitters?"

As he posed the question he waited to see if there would be any response.

"What I wish for at the moment," Shana answered him, "is to see all of Rome before we have to leave. I have read so much about the Eternal City that I shall cry if I miss any of the important statues and pictures or particularly St. Peter's."

"I thought you were in a hurry to return home," the Marquis observed as the Steward offered him a plate of fresh fish.

"That is true," Shana agreed, "so I shall have to hurry. Do be clever and make sure we do not have to spend too long with the people we are going to see."

She did not want to give them a name because there were two Stewards present in the Saloon.

The Marquis did not reply. He was merely thinking that in the sunlight her hair was so beautiful, even more than last night under the light from the golden corolla.

"What I find strange," he said, "is that you seem to know so much about the countries of Europe, but have not, I understand, visited many of them."

"I have visited them in my mind. Perhaps that is the best way to travel, as then one is never disappointed."

The Marquis laughed.

"That is certainly an idea I have never thought of before. But I like to do my sightseeing in person."

"It's always so much easier for a man," Shana said with a little sigh, thinking of her father.

"One day you will have a husband who will take you to places you want to see, or perhaps there will be someone like me who needs you urgently for an unexpected mission."

"I was thinking last night before I climbed into bed," Shana answered, "that I should to be very grateful to you. Perhaps I have been impolite in not telling you earlier how exciting it is for me to travel in this magnificent yacht and be given the chance of seeing Gibraltar and Rome."

The Marquis noticed once again that she did not say that it was wonderful to be with him.

He looked into her eyes and they were excited by what she was saying and yet he could not pretend that he saw anything personal in them when she was looking at him.

"What are we going to do this morning?" Shana asked. "Except of course stare at the view."

"I am going to challenge you to a game of deck-tennis," he said. "And if you have not played it before, I shall teach you how to."

"As it so happens, I have played deck-tennis and I rather fancy myself at the game."

"That is certainly a challenge."

The Marquis thought that as he was an expert he would score a very easy victory.

However, it would have been better not to have suggested anything so athletic for he had not counted on Shana being so quick and so observant. She always caught him out when he least anticipated it.

He won by only a hair's breadth, but it had been a much more energetic game than he had anticipated.

Shana threw herself down into a deck-chair.

"I feel much better after all that exercise, but what I would really like would be to gallop on one of your superb horses and race you on your private Racecourse."

"How do you know I have one?" the Marquis enquired.

Shana thought as she spoke that she had made a mistake.

Her father had told her that there was a Racecourse at the Hall, but owing to the old Marquis's illness it fell into a bad state of repair and he had said that one of the first things the new holder of the title should do would be to put the Racecourse in order.

"I think Bob must have told me," Shana replied

vaguely. "Perhaps it is untrue."

"No, it is true, but I am currently enlarging it and making it very much more challenging than it was before. I hope when it is finished you will come and see it."

"It sounds most exciting," Shana murmured after a short pause.

The expression in her eyes told him not only that she thought his invitation unlikely, but that she did not particularly wish to accept one.

'Now what does she mean?' the Marquis asked himself.

He thought that day by day since they had left London she had become even more of an enigma – indeed more and more difficult for him to understand.

A week ago he would have laughed scornfully if anyone had told him he was going to meet a woman who would be elusive, original and a puzzle. He would have thought that whoever made such a suggestion was talking nonsense.

If there was one matter he considered he knew all about, it was women.

Goodness knows he had had enough experience with them, but Shana never ceased to surprise him.

It was ridiculous to suppose that a girl of no consequence, who was forced to earn her own living, would be able to keep him guessing.

Yet was her family really poor? He was experienced in women's clothes and realised that everything Shana wore was well-made, fashionable and obviously expensive.

If her father could afford to buy them for her, why did she have to be a teacher? And if it was not her father, was it really possible some man could have provided them for her?

It was a question which might have puzzled him, but

last night something mystical about Shana had driven him from her cabin.

He was becoming convinced that she had never been kissed, let alone possessed by a man.

This was now the fourth day they had been together.

He thought if he was truthful that he still knew absolutely nothing about her and certainly no more than when she had come to the Hall to warn him he was about to be burgled.

She remained an enigma.

*

Because it was so warm they decided to sit on the deck after luncheon.

"I want to talk to you seriously," the Marquis began.

"What about, my Lord?"

"Yourself, for one thing."

"My life is incredibly boring," she responded. "I know all about myself and there are so many other interesting and amusing matters we could discuss."

"What sort of matters?"

"Spain first, as we are still near the South coast of that country. And then perhaps Corsica, which I suppose we shall soon pass and Napoleon Bonaparte who was born there."

She spoke expectantly.

The Marquis knew that if he behaved as he had the last few days, they would instantly have been involved in a long discussion – not only about Napoleon Bonaparte, but about war and the effect it had on the countries who suffered from it.

"Now you are deliberately trying to change the direction of my thoughts. As I have already said, I want to talk about *you*."

"In which case," Shana retorted, "I shall walk round the deck or go and talk to the Captain. He, at least, will be only too ready to talk about the *Seashell*."

"I cannot believe there is anything left for you to learn about my yacht."

"I am sure I shall find hundreds of points of interest if I trouble to look for them," Shana replied. "However, if we must be personal, we should start with you, because you are older than I am."

"Very well," the Marquis agreed reluctantly. "What do you want to know about me?"

"I should like to know about your plans for the future and what you intend to do for your estate and, I hope, for our country?"

The Marquis did not speak and she continued,

"My father is always saying it is so important, if you have something to say, to have a platform. You have one in the House of Lords. How are you going to use it?"

The Marquis was astonished as it was a question no one had ever asked him.

"How would you expect me to use my platform?" he prevaricated.

Shana thought for a moment and then she said,

"You should know better than I do that there are a great many injustices in the country and there are many people who need someone to lead them."

"What sort of people," the Marquis asked, thinking it was a question she might have difficulty in answering.

"Those who are suffering," Shana said immediately, "from poverty, illness, or simply because they do not know how to use their talents or their skills."

She looked out to sea before resuming,

"Have you ever visited the slums of London, or

listened to the complaints of those who I understand wait outside the Houses of Parliament in the hope that someone will hear them and take up their cause?"

The Marquis remained silent and Shana carried on,

"I know you have only recently come into your title, but now you are a gentleman of considerable importance and stature. As far as I can make out, there is no one to speak for the little man and who really cares whether he lives or dies, except at election time. What these people need is leadership and that is exactly what someone like you can give them."

The Marquis looked incredulous.

He was on the committee of a number of charitable organisations and gave a considerable amount of money to charity. He did not think that anything more was expected of him.

"As you have been a soldier," Shana was saying, "you know only too well that men have to be both trained and led to fight the enemy. The same need arises in civilian life."

She sighed.

"The young men have no opportunities for developing their talents and they desperately need someone to give them the right leadership and encouragement if they are ever going to achieve anything."

"I understand exactly what you are saying," the Marquis said as Shana finished. "At the same time, why me? I have my own life to lead without taking on more burdens than are absolutely necessary."

"That is a very silly question," Shana replied, "and you know the answer without my telling you. You are important, you are rich, you are young, and you have a very good brain. People will listen to you as you have influence. What other qualities do you require?"

The Marquis chuckled.

"I just do not believe it," he exclaimed. "How can you possibly, looking as you do and being so young, take me to task in a way which I find particularly difficult to refute?"

"Perhaps, after all, this voyage will not have been wasted, if I can convince you of your duty."

"How I dislike that word," the Marquis said. "It always implies something unpleasant."

"It means that you are required to give something of yourself to other people. My father has always believed that one has nothing more valuable to give than *oneself*."

"You have certainly given me a good deal to think about," the Marquis answered. "Actually I have planned to lead a quiet life in the country and not trouble myself with the problems of politics and the world outside."

"If you do, it will be a senseless waste of good material."

"I have never," the Marquis complained, "been referred to as *material* before. But I suppose one lives and learns!"

Then because he sounded as if he was really insulted by the suggestion, they both began to laugh.

"I cannot believe this conversation is taking place," the Marquis said. "Since I am finding it difficult to hold my own, I challenge you to another game of deck-tennis which I intend to win."

"I shall make sure," Shana replied, "that you do not do so too easily. I will go and change my shoes."

She ran across the deck and disappeared.

The Marquis stared after her.

How could he ever have found anyone so extraordinary? And how annoying it was to have to admit that what she was saying was entirely right – it was something he should have thought of himself.

They played their game of deck-tennis and although the Marquis won again, he had to fight hard to gain the upper hand.

*

The *Seashell* anchored in a quiet bay for the night off the coast of Corsica.

"Tomorrow we shall be in Rome," the Marquis announced as they finished dinner. "I want to tell you, Shana, I have enjoyed every moment of this voyage in a way I did not at all expect when we sailed from London."

"And I have enjoyed it so much too, it has been very exciting talking to you and arguing with you on so many absorbing subjects."

"It is something I never anticipated doing with a woman. I can only think it is a pity that you are not a man, for undoubtedly you would be challenging Mr. Gladstone as Prime Minister or perhaps Lord Granville as Secretary of State for Foreign Affairs!"

"That is just the kind of position *you* should aim at," Shana retorted, "as you know a great deal more about Europe than most people and I think the intrigues and difficulties which you would be confronted with, you would find fascinating and rewarding."

The Marquis held up his hands.

"Now you are pushing me into trouble," he complained, "and hard work. If you say very much more I shall become alarmed at what you might inveigle me into and I will have to throw you overboard to the fishes!"

Shana laughed.

"If you throw me into the sea, I shall become a water-nymph and haunt you wherever you go. You will not be able to escape me at sea and you will certainly find me in your lake when you return home!"

"You would look so lovely as a water-nymph that you are tempting me to carry out my threat!"

"I am not afraid," Shana smiled. "You pledged yourself to protect me and that means of course you must protect me from yourself."

It was what the Marquis had been thinking last night and it occurred to him that their minds were undoubtedly on a very similar wavelength.

They might in some magical way be the other half of each other.

"That is just what the Greeks believe we are all seeking in our lives," Shana chimed in.

"Now you are reading *my* thoughts," the Marquis protested.

"Just as you can read mine," Shana answered. "Perhaps we have been together in other lives. Who knows, I might have been your brother or sister?"

The Marquis noticed that she did not say 'wife.'

"Whatever we may have been," he said, "I am sure that now we have met again we have managed to air our opinions and our ideas and I find yours fascinating."

He stretched out his hand and covered hers.

"I want to look after you, Shana," he told her gently, "and I cannot contemplate you having to earn your own living in the future."

For a moment Shana could not think of anything to say.

She looked up at the Marquis and there was an expression in his eyes that she had not noticed earlier.

She could not exactly put it into words and it made her feel a little shy and almost as if her heart was turning a somersault.

She rose to her feet taking her hand away from the Marquis's.

"The Captain tells me," she said, "that we shall be sailing into the port of Ostia tomorrow morning. I do not wish to miss a moment of it, so I am retiring to my cabin."

The Marquis tried to think how he could keep her from leaving him.

Even as he hesitated, Shana had reached the door of the Saloon.

"Goodnight," she called sweetly, "and thank you for a wonderful day. It has been very exciting, but I think tomorrow will be even more so."

She was gone before he could think of a reply.

He realised instinctively it would be a mistake to follow her or to upset her in any way before they reached Rome, and he was well aware that they both faced quite an ordeal ahead of them with the Chief of the Security Police.

'She is being very brave about it,' the Marquis mused to himself, 'but I would not expect her to be anything else.'

Equally he knew the encounter was bound to be upsetting and although Shana had not said so, he knew she was apprehensive.

'We can only help them with what we know,' the Marquis decided. 'When they realise it is impossible for Shana to find the men she has seen, we will be able to go home.'

There was a question in his mind as to what 'going home' meant and because he was afraid of the answer even to himself, he did not wish to think about it.

When he finally climbed into bed he was acutely aware that she was so close to him.

Even more aware that he was finding it difficult to think of the future without her.

The *Seashell* passed into the port of Ostia where the river Tiber reaches the sea.

The Marquis was not surprised to find at breakfast that Shana knew as much about the Tiber and its turbulent history as he did.

She was talking excitedly of when Horatio had held the bridge and the Etruscan armies who had waded across the river at its shallowest point and she was eager for her first glimpse of the Eternal City.

When they disembarked there was an Officer waiting for them with a carriage to convey them to their appointment with the Chief of Police.

"This is most kind of you," the Marquis intoned as they drove off.

The Officer was sitting opposite them with his back to the horses.

"We have been waiting for you for the last few days, my Lord," the Officer began. "But even so, we expected a far longer wait. Your yacht must have been very fast."

"I like to think it is faster than almost any other ship afloat and we experienced a very comfortable voyage without any trouble through the Bay of Biscay."

The Officer smiled.

"That, I am always informed, my Lord, is a test for any vessel that ventures through it."

"Well, we passed the test and so did the *Seashell*," the Marquis replied with pride. "How are things in Rome?"

The Officer answered with a long list of the difficulties and frustrations which were making it difficult for those in authority.

Shana did not bother to listen as she was looking out

at the beauty of the countryside and eventually the City of Rome came into view.

They did not pass the Fountain of Trevi, but she asked the Officer if they were likely to do so. However there were many other fountains to be seen everywhere in Rome as on every Piazza there were fountains embellished with sculptures and elaborate marble basins, their water glistening like rainbows that made Shana's heart leap.

She knew how disappointed she would have been if Rome had not been as beautiful as in her dreams.

All too soon they drew up outside an impressive building.

The Officer escorted them up the steps and they walked along a number of lofty corridors. With a great deal of bowing and scraping, men-at-arms in glamorous uniforms showed them into a large room in the centre of which was an enormous writing table.

At it sat an elderly man in uniform wearing a large number of medals. He sprang to his feet when the Marquis was announced and walked towards him holding out his hand.

"It is a great honour, my Lord," he announced pompously, "and I cannot express our gratitude to you for coming all this distance to help us."

"Your Ambassador in London was very persuasive," the Marquis replied, "and I have brought with me as requested the lady whom you wanted to meet."

The Officer bent over Shana's hand and looked at her in a scrutinising manner which made her feel embarrassed.

"How is it possible," he asked in Italian, "that anyone so young and beautiful could possibly have come into contact with these desperados who are driving us insane with their crimes."

"That is exactly what she will tell you herself," the

Marquis answered. "But I think it important, Signor, that we confer in a small room where there is no possibility of being overheard."

Shana thought this suggestion was very sensible and the Chief of Police readily agreed.

They moved into quite a small room which was unattractively furnished and when the door was closed it seemed impossible that anyone could listen in on their deliberations.

The Chief of Police was joined by two other Officers who were obviously of high rank and they all sat in a row while Shana told them what had occurred at the *Rose and Crown*.

She became aware, as did the Marquis, that they were looking at her with admiration.

When they did address her there was almost a caressing note in their voices as they asked questions.

It was impossible for Shana to tell them anything more than she had already recounted to the Marquis.

Then it was the Marquis's turn. He explained how when Shana had come to warn him and that he had taken every precaution to capture them at the Hall and yet they had escaped.

He had never anticipated that he and his men might be sprayed with a chemical, which had not only temporarily blinded them but had made them choke.

"The same method has been used here in Italy," the Chief commented, "but of course your Lordship would not have known about their diabolical methods."

The Marquis told them that the footman they had bribed had been stabbed before they made their getaway.

The Chief of Police informed him this was a usual procedure.

"They make absolutely certain that no one can talk about them after they have left and that of course applies to a dead man."

It was then that the Chief began to talk to Shana and he explained to her that she was the only person who had ever seen the thieves without their masks.

"There must be some people who know them and can recognise them," Shana remarked.

"Their families, their friends and their confederates," the Chief said, "are all far too frightened to betray them and in any case we have not the slightest idea of where any of them are."

"It does seem extraordinary," Shana answered.

She was speaking in Italian and so was the Marquis who spoke the language well without hesitating for a word. However she could not help thinking a little conceitedly that on the whole her Italian was better than his.

The Chief then explained to Shana that he would like her to look through a number of pictures of criminals from the Police archives, some of which were drawings and some were newly invented photographs.

"We have examined the background," he continued, "of every criminal the Italian Police arrested in the last few years, but it would have been impossible for any of them to have operated with this particular gang who are terrorising not only Italy but many other countries in Europe."

"It must be a very large organisation," the Marquis commented.

"It may be and it may not be," the Chief replied. "We have gone into every detail very carefully and we think there is one boss directing perhaps a dozen men over whom he has complete and absolute control. The thieves have never been known to work in two countries at the same time and they never undertake more than two or three burglaries in the same country in the same year."

"So you think it is the same team which travels from country to country?" the Marquis asked.

"What we have concluded, my Lord, but it is entirely guesswork, is that the organisation consists of perhaps three or at the most four teams, who have been trained by their head so cleverly and so carefully that they never seem to make a mistake."

"If they did you would have caught them by now."

"We never know where they will strike next," the Chief continued.

"The only fact we do know," another Official added, "is that everyone who has a really outstanding collection of pictures, antique furniture or, most of all, silver or gold, is a prime target and the thieves will sooner or later be determined to rob them."

"Why do you think they are especially keen on silver and gold?" Shana enquired.

"Because we know they have stolen some of the finest sixteenth century goldsmith's work produced by Hans of Antwerp, goldsmith to Henry VIII."

"They stole some of *his* work!" the Marquis exclaimed.

"Unfortunately quite a considerable amount from one owner, who of course did not want his loss published in the newspapers."

"That is indeed a tragedy."

"The French," Shana remarked "must be quite pleased that Louis XIV melted the Royal plate down to pay his troops so that no silver of the period remains."

"You are right, Signorina," the Chief responded. "But there are people, whose names I cannot mention, who are fortunate enough to own some of the silver furniture which was such a feature in the Palace of Versailles, none of which survived the Revolution, but it had become fashionable amongst the French noblemen – and we do know that these thieves have managed to carry away a silver dressing table, a looking-glass, and a pair of candlesticks from one noble family."

"I can see your problem is appalling" the Marquis observed, "and we can only hope that Miss Shana will be able to recognise one of the men amongst the thieves gallery you will be showing her."

"We are not optimistic, my Lord," the Chief said, "but miracles do happen."

"Let us hope we can perform one for you," the Marquis smiled.

He felt there was nothing more to say and rose to his feet.

Almost reluctantly, because the Chief and his assistants wanted to go on talking, they moved to another room.

Here likenesses of the thieves caught in the last five years had been put on display ready for Shana to cast her eye over them.

The majority were very badly executed, but a glance at most of them told her instantly that none of them resembled the two men she had served in the *Rose and Crown*.

She hesitated over one, although the image was not really like the smaller man and not elegant enough for the taller one.

"We have sent to other Police Headquarters in the country," the Chief advised her, "for some more pictures which will be arriving tomorrow. I cannot say I have much hope of their being what we require, but we would be grateful if the Signorina would look at them as well."

"Yes, of course I will, "Shana replied, "and I am sorry I cannot give you any good news with this collection."

"We shall go on trying," the Chief answered. "But I have omitted to tell you, my Lord, that as we thought it would be a mistake for you to stay at a hotel, the Duke di Cambo has offered you his house. His Grace is away at the moment in the South of France, but his servants have instructions to look after you and of course while you are in Rome you will be under our protection."

"I am very pleased to hear it," the Marquis replied. Now, if it is possible, I would like to take the Signorina to where we are staying."

The Chief turned towards Shana.

"While you are walking round Rome, Signorina, I know you will be looking at the beauty of our City. But will you also take a good look at the men you pass? If, as we have already said, by a miracle there is someone you suspect, then we will arrest him."

"I will certainly keep my eyes wide open," Shana replied, "and we can only hope that fate will be kind enough to point us in the right direction."

The Chief smiled and thanked her and the Marquis again and they were escorted back to their carriage.

They crossed one of the famous bridges over the Tiber and came to a part of Rome where there were some very impressive private residences. When they saw where they were staying, Shana was delighted – it was a beautifully designed house with a garden which reached down to the river.

A butler and three footmen welcomed them.

The house itself was furnished with many treasures and Shana was surprised that the thieves had not tried to steal them.

The Marquis too was pleased at the accommodation that had been arranged for them.

"Actually," he said, "I was worried in case we found ourselves in an uncomfortable hotel or with a family of people who never ceased talking."

"You need not be afraid of that happening here," Shana added. "In fact I find these very large rooms rather awe-inspiring."

It was obvious the Duke's house had been furnished when the owner's taste had been in favour of heavy velvet curtains, panelled walls and large and ponderous pieces of furniture. The pictures were good, but the Marquis thought they needed cleaning.

The lighting by candles seemed somewhat inadequate after the electric light on the yacht. However he had no wish to grumble as it was obvious they would be safe and well looked after in the Duke's house and the Chief had already promised that they would be guarded and watched wherever they went.

Their luggage had already arrived from the yacht and after luncheon they explored the house.

They were walking down to the river bank when the Marquis thought it would be a mistake for them to try and do too much on the first day.

"I do so want to see the Trevi fountain," Shana insisted.

So because she was so eager, the Marquis ordered the carriage which had been put at their disposal and they drove to the Trevi.

Shana remembered it had been commissioned by the order of Pope Clement XII in 1732. It was very ornate and yet it seemed to her a little surprising that it should have achieved such a world-wide reputation.

Everyone firmly believed that the fountain brought

luck to those who threw coins into its waters. What was more, not only would one's wish be granted, but having once thrown coins into the Trevi, the visitor would inevitably return to Rome.

There were quite a few people standing around the fountain when the Marquis and Shana walked from their carriage towards it.

The Marquis drew two silver crowns out of his pocket and offered one to Shana.

She shook her head.

"No thank you – it must be my money, not yours."

"What are you going to wish for?"

"That *must* be a secret," Shana replied, "but I feel quite sure my wish will be granted."

She moved nearer to the edge of the fountain and then holding a half-crown of her own in her fingers, she closed her eyes and prayed that she and the Marquis might bring justice to the evil thieves who were causing such havoc.

Then, almost as if a voice was telling her what to do, she prayed that she might find happiness.

She had not really thought of anything for herself and happiness seemed a word to cover a multitude of wishes.

Then again, as if someone was whispering to her, she knew that what she really wanted was love – the love her father and mother had known together. The love she had read about, the love which men and women had strived for since the beginning of time.

She looked up at the statue of Neptune and threw her coin glistening in the sun into the sparkling water.

She had a strong feeling as it fell that it was her last wish that went with it – the wish that concerned herself.

The Marquis was standing beside her and now he took her arm.

"I am taking you back to the house," he said. "We have done enough for one day and I am trying to believe that my wish will come true."

"But of course it will and I believe that mine will too."

"Can I guess what that is?" the Marquis asked coyly.

"No. *No!* I am sure that would be unlucky. It would undoubtedly annoy the Gods who listen to us before our coins touch the water."

"Then I devoutly hope they were listening to my wish," the Marquis said.

He waited for Shana to ask him what it was and felt almost absurdly disappointed because she did not seem to be interested.

CHAPTER SIX

They enjoyed a delicious dinner served in the Duke's austere and rather overwhelming dining room.

When it was over they walked down the garden to look again at the river, which was very glamorous with lights from small barges moving on the water.

The Marquis became acutely aware he wanted to hold Shana close in his arms and kiss her. He was however sure that she must be tired as it had been a long and difficult day and he told himself that he must not rush his fences.

When they turned back to the house Shana confirmed, as he had expected, that she was feeling weary.

"It was not as difficult as I had feared talking to the Chief of Police and those other Officers," she said. "At the same time I was frightened of making a mistake."

"I thought you were splendid and we certainly cannot tell them what we do not know."

"Of course not and frankly I am beginning to think that those Italians thieves are far too clever ever to be caught."

She gave a little sigh and walked upstairs with the Marquis to their bedrooms.

Shana was glad to see that she was near the Marquis.

What they had been given, she realised, was really a suite at the end of a long corridor and when they entered the suite they found themselves in a very comfortable drawing room or boudoir. The Marquis's bedroom was on one side of it and hers on the other.

"I am so glad I am looking over the river," Shana said as they entered the suite.

"I think I prefer to overlook the garden," the Marquis replied. "I shall not be woken with hoots from the barges."

"Now you are trying to spoil my fun, so I shall just say goodnight as I expect we will have another difficult day tomorrow."

"I am afraid so and we told the Chief we would be with him fairly early in the morning."

Shana sighed and said,

"I looked at hundreds of their drawings and photographs and I cannot believe there are many more suspects left in Italy!"

"I do hope you are right. Goodnight, Shana, and sleep well."

She smiled at him and walked across to the door into her room.

Once again the Marquis wondered what would happen if he came after her and kissed her goodnight, but resolutely he forced himself to go to his own room.

He had deliberately told Curtis not to wait up for him as he had half hoped that he would be able to talk to Shana more intimately. Perhaps they would have been able to sit together in the drawing room for some time before they actually retired.

'It is no use making plans,' the Marquis told himself angrily. "I shall have to wait and see. Perhaps when we have left Rome it will be easier.'

He decided that once they had completed their mission, he would persuade Shana to travel with him a little further across the Mediterranean.

He knew that she wanted to visit Greece and perhaps it would be a temptation she could not resist.

He kept remembering however that she wanted to be home before her father returned and that obviously might make her determined to go back to England immediately the Police no longer required their presence in Rome.

All these thoughts surged through his mind and once again it was a long time before he fell asleep.

*

In the morning they breakfasted in their drawing room before setting out again for the offices of the Chief of Police.

When they arrived he told them triumphantly that he had collected photographs and drawings of every criminal called Abramo.

The Marquis looked surprised and the Chief explained,

"It means Abraham, my Lord, in your language and it's quite a common name in this part of Italy."

Shana was taken into the room where the photographs and drawings had been laid out.

She inspected them closely, but thinking that whatever anyone else might think it was a waste of time. As the two Italians had been clever enough not to be captured by the Marquis and his men, it was extremely unlikely that they would have been in the hands of the Italian Police at any time.

However, there were so many Abramos that it was nearly luncheon time before they were finally able to leave and Shana was totally unable to find even the slightest resemblance to the men she had seen.

"You must promise, Signorina," the Chief urged Shana as they were about to depart, "that you will continue to look around you wherever you go. I cannot believe that you have come all this way to help us and we should be so unlucky that you will leave us without any positive result."

"I will do my best, Signor," Shana promised, "but I am afraid the Gods are against us."

"That I will not accept," the Chief answered, "when you yourself, Signorina, look just like one of the Goddesses in the National Museum."

Shana thanked him for the compliment and after such a comment the Marquis insisted that the carriage take them to the National Museum. He thought there may indeed be some resemblance to Shana in a head of Venus which he had heard had been found in the Tiber.

They entered the museum and walked down several corridors before stopping in front of the statue of the Capitoline Venus.

It was a beautiful statue with the Goddess represented in the act of stepping into her bath and they both looked at her face to see if there was any resemblance to Shana.

The Marquis was trying hard not to think of her nakedness and Shana at the same time.

"If you find the men the Chief is seeking," he mused, "I am quite certain they will place a statue of you in one of the museum rooms and I cannot believe that you will not look even more beautiful than the Venus I see here."

Shana blushed at the Marquis's words.

She looked round and observed that most of the statues were of men and told him,

"I think that we shall have to go to Greece if we want to see a really beautiful Venus or rather Aphrodite."

The Marquis knew this was true, but he did not say at the moment that was where he was hoping to take her.

"I cannot think why you are so interested in the Colosseum," the Marquis said when they arrived. "It was designed to hold 80,000 spectators watching what I should think was a most unpleasant spectacle of men and women being savaged by wild beasts and gladiators fighting each other to the death."

"I was not thinking of the games," Shana chided him, "but the legend that as long as the Colosseum stands Rome will stand, but when Rome falls, so will the world."

"It seems to be standing up at the moment," the Marquis remarked sardonically.

Shana did not answer.

She was looking down to where thousands of early Christians had been martyred.

Impulsively she turned away.

"You are right. It is not a happy place and I do not like to dwell on what has happened here in the past."

The Marquis took her to a very good restaurant for luncheon and when they had finished he suggested that they should return to the house.

"I am going to take you out to dinner tonight to where I am told they serve the best food in the whole of Rome. So I do not want you to be tired or tell me when we get there that you are not hungry."

Shana laughed.

"I am always hungry and it sounds very exciting."

After she had explored some of the rooms she had not seen earlier, they went up to their own drawing room and by this time it was late in the afternoon and Shana agreed that she would rest before dinner.

"That is an excellent idea," the Marquis said, "and as I need some fresh air I am going to walk along by the river."

Shana heard him close the door of the drawing room.

She wished she was going with him and then she told

herself she was sure that at times, like her father, the Marquis liked to be alone.

Curtis arranged for her to have a bath in her bedroom and two footmen carried the hot water upstairs.

She chose one of her prettiest evening gowns to wear for dinner with the Marquis and hoped he would think her as smart as some of the beauties he had dined with in London or in the country. She had a shawl to drape over her shoulders if it was cool in the carriage.

When she joined the Marquis in the drawing room he thought she was lovelier than any Venus he had ever seen.

The Duke's comfortable carriage took them to the restaurant which was at the far end of the City.

The Marquis had been correctly advised that it was the best food in Rome.

Shana enjoyed it all, especially seeing the other diners. Most of the ladies were very smart with the gentlemen in evening dress.

She noticed that she and the Marquis caused a number of whispered comments as they entered the restaurant and once they were seated several people asked the Head Waiter who they were.

She did not think they were looking at her particularly as the Marquis was not only handsome but taller than all the other men present.

They sat talking until the restaurant was beginning to empty and as it was now late they asked their driver to take them straight back to the Duke's house.

There was still quite a lot of traffic in the streets of Rome and just as they were approaching the house, the horses came to a standstill.

Shana was looking out of the window on her side of the carriage and saw a man coming down the flight of steps of an impressive looking house.

He had almost reached them when she gave a gasp.

"What is it?" the Marquis enquired.

"*That man*! Look at him!" Shana cried.

Even as she spoke the man had almost reached their carriage.

He looked directly at Shana through the open window before turning away.

The Marquis bent over her.

"What man?" he asked.

"There. That man over there. I am almost sure it was the Italian in the *Rose and Crown*, who was better educated than his companion."

"Can you be certain? You cannot have seen him very clearly."

"The light from the carriage lamp was on his face and there is also a moon."

"If you are certain it is he, then we will have to tell the Chief of Police at once."

"We can describe the house he was leaving," Shana suggested and the Marquis agreed.

She knew as they drove on that the Marquis could hardly believe that the man she had just seen was actually the man who had been in the *Rose and Crown*.

Now she had seen him again, Shana vaguely remembered that she had noticed at the time that one of his eyelids drooped more than the other and his nose was thin and pointed.

'I am quite sure it was him,' she said to herself.

Because the Marquis was doubtful, she did not go on talking about him.

At the same time she was almost certain he had recognised her. In which case, she thought, he will disappear and will certainly not be at that house tomorrow if the Chief of Police goes to arrest him.

There seemed to be no point in discussing the encounter further, so when they went upstairs Shana told herself she would go to bed and think about it all when tomorrow came.

The candles were lit in their drawing room and there was an oil lamp so that the room seemed quite bright, but the passages had been nearly dark and Shana suddenly felt the house was rather gloomy.

"I am so glad," she said to the Marquis, "that you are next door. I think it is rather creepy being in this big house all by ourselves."

"There are plenty of servants downstairs."

"Yes, but they are a long way from us."

The Marquis smiled.

"I promised I would look after you," he assured her, "and that is what I shall do. Go to bed, Shana and forget that man until tomorrow."

"I will try and you are just across the room – "

"I tell you what we will do," the Marquis suggested, "we will leave our doors open. If you need me you have only to cry out and I shall hear you."

Shana nodded.

"It sounds rather foolish, but it would make me happy."

"Then that is what we will do and do not forget we have a special guard in attendance. I spoke to him this afternoon and he told me he had just come on duty and there would be another man taking over from him early tomorrow morning."

"That sounds very grand," Shana exclaimed.

"Then go to bed and sleep well. And just call out if you want me."

She thanked him and walked into her own room.

When the Marquis entered his room, he was frowning. He had made light of what Shana had said about seeing the Italian.

If she was right it could mean trouble.

He took his revolver out of the dressing table drawer where Curtis had left it on his instructions and loaded it.

He hesitated and then walking across the room placed it under his pillow.

*

Shana undressed, thinking how kind the Marquis was to her and what an exciting evening it had been. There had been so much to talk about and somehow they had quite forgotten the reason they were in Rome.

They had discussed what he might do in the future and instead of arguing with her the Marquis had listened to everything she had to say. She had thought it very complimentary that he had been so interested in all her suggestions.

'It is very wonderful being with him,' Shana thought as she blew out the lights by her bed.

Usually she would read a little before falling asleep, but tonight she wanted to think about the Marquis and everything they had talked about over dinner.

She must have been asleep for several hours.

Suddenly she was conscious that someone was bending over her.

For a second she thought it might be the Marquis and then she realised it was not him and was about to scream.

Before she could do so, something soft but firm covered her mouth and she realised she was being gagged.

Now she began to struggle frantically.

She was pulled forward and the gag was fastened behind her head.

Although she fought hard against her attacker, her arms were pulled down on each side and a strong rope bound them tight.

Next her feet were being tied together and again she tried to scream but it was impossible.

She knew it was a man tying her up, but the room was in darkness and she could not make out his features.

Now frantic and terrified she wanted to cry for the Marquis and as it was impossible to make a sound she could only call to him silently.

'Help me! *Help me*! Come to me. I am being kidnapped!'

Even as the cry went out from her as silently as a prayer, she was suddenly enveloped in what she thought must be a sheet or a rug that covered her completely. It was held in place by more strong cords like those already binding her.

"*Come to me*! *Come to me*! *Save me*! *Save me*!"

She fervently believed that the Marquis must be able to hear her inaudible screams.

Then as she felt herself being picked up by a man's strong arms she knew she was lost.

*

The Marquis had been unable to sleep because he was thinking of Shana.

As he was just dozing off he suddenly sensed that she was calling to him. It was loud cry or so he thought.

He sat up in bed.

Then he realised there was only silence and it must have been his imagination.

But still in some strange way he could feel that she wanted him and she was, in fact, calling for him. It was so clear that he thought he could not be imagining it.

He climbed out of bed and pulled on his robe which Curtis had left lying over a chair.

Taking his revolver from under the pillow, he walked through the open door into the drawing room.

After Shana had retired to bed he had blown out all the candles, but had left the oil lamp, which was quite a small one, burning on the writing table and so he could easily see the way to her room.

He had no wish to frighten her and therefore moved quietly across the thick carpet thinking that if she was asleep he would not waken her.

He pushed open the door which was slightly ajar and saw at once that the curtains over the window had been pulled back.

A man who appeared to be carrying Shana was in the act of handing her out of the window to a confederate outside.

Just for a moment the Marquis paused.

Then he shot the man who was holding Shana in the back.

As the explosion seemed to fill the whole room he fell forward and the man outside the window took the sudden force of Shana's feet.

He gave a scream and disappeared and as he did so the Marquis rushed forward and caught hold of Shana, who might have fallen either way off the windowsill.

The Marquis picked her up in his arms and realised how completely she was enveloped and bound.

He carried her across the drawing room and into his own bedroom where he laid her gently on the bed.

Next he ran back into Shana's room, where he picked up the man he had shot and threw him out of the window and when he had done so he looked out to see where he had fallen.

The moonlight showed very clearly that there were two men spread-eagled on the ground below and the Marquis thought that the one he had shot was dead.

At least as they had both fallen on a tiled path, they would be unconscious from concussion and he noticed that the man who had been outside the window had fallen from a rope ladder that had been fastened to the windowsill.

He had intended to carry Shana down over his shoulder just like as a fire-fighter and the other man would have followed and the Marquis realised that they must have practised this well-executed performance many times to be so efficient.

He released the rope ladder so that it fell to the ground on top of the prostrate men and closed the window before returning to his own room.

Shana was still lying on the bed where he had left her.

Very gently he untied the ropes which held the sheet covering her and then when she could see him vaguely in the moonlight coming from the uncurtained window he undid her gag.

As he looked down at her frightened face he realised she was trembling violently.

He bent his head.

"It is all right, my darling," he said, "you are safe and no one shall take you away again."

As he finished speaking he kissed her very gently.

As his mouth held her lips captive, he felt that she responded to him.

Quickly he began to undo the ropes around her arms

and ankles and only as he finished did she say in a voice which was little more than a whisper,

"You – came. You – heard me."

"I heard you calling me," the Marquis told her. "Now you needn't be frightened anymore. The men are dead."

He put his arms around her as he spoke and he would have kissed her again, but she burst into tears.

She hid her face against his neck and he held her very close.

"It is all over, my precious, my darling. You are safe and nothing like this shall ever happen to you again."

She was still trembling and as she was wearing only her nightgown the Marquis thought she might be cold.

He pulled open the bedclothes and laid Shana down into the bed with her head on the pillow and then he covered her.

Her hands came out to hold onto him.

"I – thought they – were – going to – kill me," she managed to stutter.

"You were absolutely right in believing it was the man you had seen at the inn and I was wrong," the Marquis admitted. "You will have to forgive me for being so foolish."

"How could – they have – worked so – quickly?" Shana stammered.

"They have obviously had a great deal of experience. The way they climbed up to your window was the work of experts."

"I thought – they would – kill me," Shana whispered again.

"No one shall kill you, my beautiful one," the Marquis said lovingly.

Then he was kissing her again, kissing her lips and the tears away from her eyes and her cheeks.

When he finally raised his head she gave a little cry.

"*Don't – leave – me!*"

"I have no intention of doing so, my dearest Shana, but I want you to go to sleep and forget what has happened."

He kissed her again and now he realised that she was no longer trembling.

Her lips were soft and sweet against his and he was also aware of how innocent she was.

He was certain that he was the first man who had ever kissed her.

"I want you to try to go to sleep, my precious. You know as well as I do that we are going to have a difficult time tomorrow explaining all that has happened tonight."

He thought it very likely that the men who had come to kidnap Shana would first have attacked their guard, but he did not want Shana to know.

He closed the door into the drawing room and locked it.

Then he moved to the other side of the bed and realised that Shana was watching him.

He lay down beside her still wearing his robe and pulled the eiderdown, which he had dispensed with when he got into bed, over them both.

"Now I am here," he assured her, "and my revolver is still loaded if anyone interrupts us."

"I am still – frightened of what they – could do," Shana murmured.

"I think the two men were on their own, although there will be others waiting for them. But when they do not appear, there will be nothing more they can do tonight."

"And you – will stay – with – me?" Shana asked.

"This is my bed," the Marquis smiled, "and just as I want you to go to sleep, I need some rest too."

She stretched out her hand and held onto the lapel of his robe.

"You do not – think that they will try – to kill us – both?"

"I think they would like to, but it will be very difficult to break in now that my door is locked and I doubt if they could conjure up another means on this side of the house to carry us both away."

He spoke so firmly that Shana seemed reassured.

At the same time she did not stop holding on to him.

The Marquis slipped his arm round her and drew her closer.

"Now you are safe," he whispered softly, "and although I want to go on kissing you, my precious, I want you to sleep."

He kissed her once again.

Then although he longed to be closer still to her, he closed his eyes, recognising that the shock of what had just happened would have left most women screaming hysterically.

Shana's self-control prevented her from behaving like other women and yet inevitably she would suffer a reaction from the terror she had just been through.

He knew he was right when ten minutes later he realised that she was fast asleep – the sleep of utter exhaustion.

*

Shana was still asleep when the rising sun came through the window.

The Marquis lay watching the first beam touch Shana's golden hair.

Now that he could see her face quite clearly, he knew

no one could look lovelier even after all that she had gone through.

He lay looking at her thinking that she was unique in every way. It would have been impossible for any woman to have behaved better in such appalling circumstances.

A little later he thought he heard the drawing room door open.

Very gently he managed to take his arm from behind Shana without waking her and then moving silently towards the door he unlocked it and entered the drawing room.

He was right in thinking that someone was there – it was Curtis, who would have spoken, but the Marquis put his finger to his lips and Curtis understood.

The Marquis closed the door into his own room and crossed into Shana's and beckoned Curtis to follow him.

Once inside he signalled to him to close the door before he asked,

"What has happened?"

"Terrible things, my Lord," Curtis replied. "Three men dead, and the guard who 'as just come on duty 'as gone back to fetch his Chief."

"I expected this to have happened," the Marquis said. "The two men they found dead beneath the window were trying to abduct Miss Shana and I guessed they must have killed our guard first."

"Stabbed 'im through the 'eart, my Lord, 'e be a nasty sight I can tell you."

"I do not doubt it and how long ago did the guard who has just come on duty leave for his Headquarters?"

"Over fifteen minutes ago, my Lord. I was asleep when 'e arrived and 'e wakes the other servants and as soon as he'd done so and afore us were dressed, he sets orf."

"Then he should be back very soon. I will fetch my

clothes and you can help me dress. However, I wish Miss Shana to sleep as long as possible."

He did not wait for Curtis to reply, but returned to his bedroom and very quickly collected his clothes.

Shana did not stir.

The Marquis was determined to keep all this trouble from her for as long as possible and to make it easier for her when she had to report what had occurred.

He had just finished dressing when the Duke's butler entered the drawing room. Curtis heard him and managed to push him into Shana's bedroom before he could speak.

"I was just coming downstairs," the Marquis told him.

"I came to tell you, my Lord," the butler blurted out, "that the Chief of Police is here with three of his men. I have put them in the Saloon and they said they would like some coffee."

"I will come at once, "the Marquis said briskly. "But we will leave Curtis here in case Miss Shana wakes up and finds herself alone."

He looked at Curtis as he spoke and knew there was no necessity to give any other instructions.

The Marquis walked quickly downstairs and the Chief of Police rose to his feet as he entered the Saloon.

"I expect you have been told," the Marquis began, "exactly what happened last night."

"I have seen the bodies, my Lord," the Chief answered, "and I am horrified. Can you explain how this has happened?"

"I can do so easily. My cousin, Miss Brooke, thought she recognised one of the men we are looking for coming down the steps of a house while our carriage was held up by traffic in the road last night."

"Coming from a house! Do you know which house it

was?"

"It is easy to describe. It was the last house before we reached the road which brings us here beside the river."

The Chief stared at him and the Marquis continued,

"It has nearly a dozen steps up to the front door which is most impressive. I noticed when we were driving yesterday that the house itself was built of black bricks and the owner, I should have thought, must be an individual of some distinction."

"Black bricks!" the Chief exclaimed in an astonished voice. "But it cannot be Labrama!"

The Marquis stared at him.

"Labrama?" he asked. "Why did you not think of that name before? Miss Shana said Abramo was as near as she could get to the name mentioned by the Italians in England."

"Palazzo Labrama, my Lord," the Chief said slowly, "is the home of Prince Vasaro."

His two companions had remained silent, but now they joined in the conversation.

One of them said the Prince had always been a recluse and the other informed them that it was well known that he owned a magnificent art collection.

Some of it was inherited and some he had bought during his lifetime.

"And the rest he has been stealing!" the Chief intervened. "Now I understand many clues which I should have considered earlier. The reports of large van loads of what appeared to be furniture being taken to the Palazzo. The rumours that the Prince never entertained nor invited any of his acquaintances in Rome to visit him."

They were still talking nineteen to the dozen when the Marquis interrupted,

"I think, Chief, that we have now solved your

problem. May I ask that my cousin be involved in your investigation as little as possible? I think it would be best if I made a statement on her behalf. Then there would be no need for her to be cross-questioned any more. The man you were looking for is dead and his body is now in your possession."

"I can understand exactly what you are saying, my Lord," the Chief replied. "And I can promise that your very beautiful cousin will not be troubled any further. If your Lordship will make a full statement of everything that occurred last night, that will be sufficient for us to act on, as I intend to do immediately."

There was fortunately a large desk in the Saloon and the Marquis sat down.

He wrote his report in Italian as he thought it would save time and signed his name with a flourish.

The Marquis was well aware, because Prince Vasaro was so important, that the Chief of Police would be praised and congratulated on solving such a difficult criminal case and it would be to his advantage if the announcement was handled discreetly.

When he handed over his report the Chief thanked him profusely for everything he had done.

"I can only speak on behalf of all my people, my Lord, when I tell you how grateful we are. I know you will have the gratitude of a great many other countries in Europe, especially France."

"To prove your gratitude, I should be most grateful if you do not reveal my name or that of my cousin. Take the credit, Chief, of having found this man yourself and please keep us completely out of the picture."

The Marquis caught a flicker of delight in the Chief's eyes as he recognised that it would do him a great deal of good if everyone believed that it was his brilliance alone that had tracked down the Prince Vasaro and his evil gang.

He decided to give the Chief a considerable donation for the Police benefit fund, which pleased him a great deal and then he left them to enjoy their breakfast.

He ran upstairs and into his bedroom.

Shana was still asleep, but she stirred as she heard him open the door.

"What has happened?" she asked drowsily.

The Marquis walked across the room and sat down on the bed.

He bent forward and kissed her.

"It is all over," he told her. "We will need to pay a visit to the British Embassy and then we can leave Rome."

The memory of what had happened last night flooded over Shana and she reached out her hands towards him.

"That man – tried to take me away," she mumbled a little incoherently.

"It has all to be forgotten," the Marquis said quietly. "The Chief of Police has everything he needs in his hands and the man you identified is now dead. He came from the Palazzo Labrama, which is owned by the Prince Vasaro."

Shana gave a gasp as the Marquis went on,

"They understand now why the Prince never entertained and kept himself very much to himself, or rather to the amazing collection of art he has stolen from so many different collectors and museums in different countries."

"You are making it all sound like a fairy story!" Shana exclaimed.

"And you are the good fairy or rather the angel of the story. Now get up and get dressed. We will have breakfast here by ourselves before proceeding to the Embassy."

He did not wait for her to ask any more questions, but walked back into the drawing room.

Curtis came in carrying a can of hot water and asked Shana which dress she would like to wear.

"I'm packin' all your other things, miss," he said, "so it'd be best if you dressed in here where there's plenty of room."

"Are we really able to go away now?" Shana asked.

"Just leave it to 'is Lordship," Curtis said cheerily, 'e's got it all under control and there's no one who can solve things better than when 'e's up against it, so to speak."

Shana laughed because she could not help it.

"That's just what I want to do as soon as possible," she said and knew it to be the truth.

CHAPTER SEVEN

Shana was dressed except for her gown and she had finished combing her hair when Curtis knocked and came into the room.

"I've packed all your other things, miss," he announced, "and 'is Lordship thought you'd like to wear this gown." He held up one as he spoke.

Shana smiled.

It was the gown she had bought thinking she might have to attend some important luncheon with her father or a fashionable garden party.

She had not worn it since she had come abroad and thought it was rather a strange choice for the Marquis to make.

However, as everything else was packed, it was no use protesting and she therefore put on the gown and Curtis did it up for her. There was a matching hat which was particularly becoming.

She realised when she walked into the drawing room that the Marquis was looking at her with admiration.

"We must hurry," he urged, "because I want to put to sea as soon as possible."

"That is just what I would like too," Shana replied.

They thanked the servants who had looked after them

and the Marquis had already tipped them generously.

When they drove off Shana gave a deep sigh of relief. She never wanted to see the bedroom again or even think of what had happened last night.

The horses took them at a good pace through the streets of Rome and when they were close to the British Embassy they came to a standstill.

The Marquis opened the door without waiting for the footman to descend from the box to do it for him.

"I will not keep you long," he called cheerfully, "I want to buy something here."

He disappeared into a shop, which Shana saw was a flower shop.

She wondered what he was doing, but thought perhaps he was buying some flowers to take with them to the *Seashell*.

The Marquis did not take long and he returned to the carriage with a large bouquet of white lilies.

As he climbed in beside Shana he placed the bouquet on her lap.

"Are these for me?" she asked. "How wonderful! I adore lilies."

"I always understood that lilies were the correct flower for a bride."

She looked at him wondering what he meant and he said gently,

"We are going to be married before we leave for our honeymoon."

Shana stared at him in sheer amazement and then she began to murmur incoherently,

"But you – cannot – marry me – without – "

Before she could say any more the carriage came to a

halt outside the British Embassy and servants ran down the steps to open the carriage door.

The Marquis climbed out.

As he helped her, Shana thought she must be dreaming.

The Marquis was so important and as everyone had said so fastidious.

How was it possible he was planning to marry a woman whom he believed to be of so little social importance that she was forced to earn her own living?

'I must tell him who I am,' Shana thought.

Her next thought was that it was the most wonderful thing that could ever have happened to her.

She was marrying a man who loved her for herself.

This was the love she had always dreamt of and had actually wished for as her coin had splashed into the Trevi Fountain.

They walked in through the Embassy door and the Marquis spoke to an *aide-de-camp* who had hurried forward when he saw them arrive.

"I would like to see His Excellency as soon as possible," he said.

"We received your message, my Lord," the *aide-de-camp* replied, "and His Excellency will be ready in a few minutes. The visitor who is with him at the moment is just about to leave."

He led the way into a very comfortable and well furnished anteroom.

Shana put her lilies down on a table and was just about to sit down when the door at the end of the room opened.

She guessed it led into the private offices of the Ambassador, who emerged in the company of another man.

When he saw the Marquis, the Ambassador smiled and held out his hand.

"I am delighted to see you, my Lord," he began.

As he spoke Shana gave a little scream.

"*Papa!*"

She ran across the room and as she flung herself against Lord Hallam, he exclaimed in astonishment,

"Shana! My dearest, what are you doing here? How is it possible you are in Rome?"

He bent to kiss his daughter and her arms were round his neck as the Ambassador and the Marquis stared at them in surprise.

Then as if the Ambassador finally found his voice he said,

"I do not know if you have met the Marquis of Kilbrooke."

Still with one arm round Shana, Lord Hallam replied,

"We are neighbours and I knew your father for many years."

"Of course I know all about you," the Marquis said, "but I had no idea that Shana was your daughter."

"Yet she is with you?" Lord Hallam queried.

The Marquis looked at the Ambassador.

"I think, Your Excellency, "that as we have a story to tell both to Lord Hallam and to you it would be wise to go into your office."

"Yes, of course," the Ambassador agreed. "Please come in and allow me to offer you some refreshment."

"I think our stories should come first," the Marquis suggested.

Holding on to her father's hand, Shana sat down on the chair beside him.

"I have had many surprises in my life," Lord Hallam said, "but this is certainly one I did not expect. I thought, Shana my dearest, that you were looking after our horses and in my wildest dreams I would not have expected to find you here in Rome!"

"It makes everything perfect that you are here, Papa, but I think perhaps I had better start from the very beginning and tell you the whole story."

"It is certainly something I would like to hear."

The Marquis and Lord Hallam had both seated themselves in armchairs and next Shana started in a small voice,

"It all happened because you told me to take – Bob Grimes the tobacco – you had bought for him."

Her father was listening intently and she went on to relate how Mrs. Grimes had fractured her leg.

In order to help out Bob, who was so excited at having someone as important as the Marquis to patronise the *Rose and Crown*, she had cooked the luncheon for the shooting party.

Because she felt shy at what she was saying, she did not look at the Marquis, but carried on to explain how the next day she had visited Mrs. Grimes and again she had cooked luncheon, only this time for the two Italians, overhearing their conversation through the false window in the passage.

"When you heard their plot," Lord Hallam interrupted, "you knew you had to warn the Marquis."

"I thought it was the only thing I could do," Shana answered. "At the same time I had no idea then how dangerous they were."

She shivered as she spoke and the Marquis said,

"I would like, my Lord, to intervene here. The rest of

the story is really mine and I will explain why I persuaded Shana to come to Rome with me."

He paused for a moment before he continued,

"I have already sent a messenger to His Excellency asking him to make arrangements for your daughter and me to be married as soon as I have informed him of what occurred here last night."

"*Married*!" Lord Hallam ejaculated.

"I have loved Shana for what now seems a very long time," the Marquis answered, "and I believe that she loves me. And I have the honour of asking you, my Lord, for your daughter's hand."

Shana gave a little murmur,

"I do – love him, Papa, I love – him with all my – heart."

Lord Hallam was used to the unexpected and in this instance his composure did not desert him.

He nodded his head and there was just a slight pause before he muttered,

"I hope I shall be allowed to give away the bride."

"Of course you must, Papa," Shana told him, "and it makes everything so wonderful for me that you will be here. But I have only just been told what has been planned."

"There is a reason for so much speed," the Marquis said. "I now want to suggest, because I do not wish Shana to be upset by hearing my report of the events since we arrived in Rome, that with your Excellency's approval she should adjourn elsewhere until your Chaplain is ready for us."

The Ambassador understood and rose to his feet.

"I will take the future bride to my wife," he suggested, "as I know she will not only look after her, but will enjoy the excitement and romance of a wedding here in the Embassy

Chapel. We have not had one for quite some time."

Shana rose and put both her arms around her father's neck and kissed him again.

"I love you, Papa," she said, "and please understand that, although what I have done may seem somewhat strange, I thought all the time it was what you would wish me to do."

She did not wait for her father's answer, but walked towards the door which the Ambassador opened for her.

As she passed the Marquis he reached out to take her hand and raised it to his lips and she knew as he did so that he was telling her with his heart that he loved her.

The Ambassador led Shana into the private part of the Embassy.

His wife, Lady Matheson, was in the drawing room sitting at her writing table and when her husband came in she rose to her feet.

She looked at the girl who was accompanying him a little questioningly.

"I have brought you, my dear, the bride we spoke about this morning who turns out to be the daughter of Lord Hallam. The Marquis has asked if you will be kind enough to look after her and help her prepare for the wedding."

"Of course I am delighted to look after her," Lady Matheson answered.

She was a good-looking woman of about fifty and there was a friendliness and warmth about her to which Shana immediately responded.

Knowing Shana would be in good hands, the Ambassador returned to his office without further ado.

While he was away, the Marquis had said to Lord Hallam,

"You must forgive me, my Lord, if this comes to you

as something of a shock. But I assure you that all I am concerned with at the moment is getting Shana away from Rome. When I tell you and the Ambassador what has happened, you will understand."

Lord Hallam smiled.

"I understand that you and Shana are in love with each other and that is more important than anything else."

"I realise now," the Marquis told him, "that I have never in my whole life been in love before now and I promise you I will make Shana happy."

"That is all that really matters."

"I am afraid that because she admires and loves you so much," the Marquis added, "she will worry that she has left you alone."

There was a short pause before Lord Hallam replied,

"I have a solution to that problem. I do not pretend that I would not have found it very lonely if I had returned home, as I intend to do, to find Shana was not there."

The Marquis did not speak and he went on,

"While I was in Paris these last weeks, I met a friend I had known many years ago who, although it seems unbelievable, has never given her heart to anyone."

Lord Hallam paused and the Marquis guessed what was coming.

"All I shall say is that I am going back to Paris and, if Shana worries too much about me, tell her you think I shall not be returning to England alone!"

"This news certainly makes matters very much easier than I thought they would be," the Marquis admitted candidly.

The door opened and the Ambassador joined them again.

"My wife is only too delighted to look after your daughter," he said to Lord Hallam.

Then turning to the Marquis saying,

"You know as well as I do that I am finding it hard to repress my curiosity about what happened last night."

The Marquis sat down.

He told Lord Hallam first, as the Ambassador had already heard this part of the story, what had happened at Brooke Hall.

How the thieves had escaped by spraying him and his men with a chemical and had killed the footman they had bribed to let them in and explained how it had been impossible, since Shana was the only person who had ever seen any of the thieves, to refuse to bring her to Rome to meet the Chief of Police.

"She examined hundreds if not thousands of drawings and photographs of known thieves, especially men called Abramo," he said. "Then last night our carriage was held up in the road and she recognised one of the men who had been at the *Rose and Crown* coming down the steps of a large house."

The Ambassador gave a loud exclamation.

"She actually saw him coming out of a house?" he quizzed. "Where was it?"

"The Chief of Police recognised it as Palazzo Labrama."

The Ambassador stared as if he felt he could not have heard correctly.

"The home of Prince Vasaro!" he exclaimed. "I do not believe it!"

"Unfortunately it is true and the man Shana saw had simultaneously seen her."

He then recounted what had happened later that night

and how only by the mercy of God he had heard Shana calling for him silently.

"I shot the man who was lifting her out through the window," he said quietly, "and would have shot the other man if he had not fallen backwards and, I gather, broke his neck."

"I have never heard of anything so fantastic," Lord Hallam commented.

"You will receive the gratitude not only of Rome, but of museums and collectors of art all over the world," the Ambassador added.

The Marquis smiled.

"I made a bargain with the Chief of Police that both my name, and of course Shana's, should be kept out of his report. He will take all the credit and now you will understand why I must leave Rome immediately."

"You do not trust the Chief of Police?" Lord Hallam asked.

"It is not a matter of not trusting him. He will be put under great pressure by people who cannot contain their curiosity. There is now nothing more that Shana or I can do and I cannot allow her to be upset again as she was last night."

His voice deepened and he looked at Lord Hallam as he said,

"I know of no other woman I have ever met who would have been so brave after such a terrifying ordeal when she knew, as you and I know, they would undoubtedly have killed her."

"I am very proud of my daughter," Lord Hallam sighed. "And you are quite right, you must depart from Rome immediately."

"I am taking her to Greece where I believe she has

always wanted to go. And now that we shall not have to worry about you, my Lord, we will have a very long honeymoon."

"I know that I can leave Shana safely in your hands," Lord Hallam smiled.

The Ambassador moved to the door and an *aide-de-camp* spoke to him.

"Everything is ready in the Chapel," he announced, "and a message has been sent to my wife."

The Ambassador took the Marquis and Lord Hallam to the back door of the Embassy and just across the courtyard there was the Chapel which had been built over a hundred years earlier.

"I hope, my Lord, you will allow me to be your Best Man," the Ambassador proposed.

"I shall be honoured, your Excellency."

He handed the Ambassador his signet ring and they walked towards the Chapel, leaving Lord Hallam to wait for Shana.

She joined him two minutes later holding her bouquet of lilies.

She was wearing a veil which Lady Matheson had worn at her own wedding and to hold it in place there was a wreath of white orchids, which the two women had made quickly.

Shana looked more beautiful than her father had ever seen her and he believed, just as the Marquis had, that there was something ethereal and different about her.

It was something he could not explain in words.

Her veil did not cover her face but fell on either side almost down to the floor.

Her eyes were shining and she looked so very lovely and Lord Hallam thought the Marquis was exceedingly lucky to have such a beautiful bride.

He gave Shana his arm and they walked slowly across the courtyard.

"It makes everything perfect that you are here, Papa," Shana whispered.

"That is just what I was thinking myself," her father replied.

The Chapel was small but beautiful and there was an abundance of flowers on the altar.

As the Marquis saw Shana arrive he thought this was exactly the wedding he wanted as there were no friends appraising the bride or giving them presents they did not require.

What mattered was that he had found the woman he did not believe existed, yet who had been part of his dreams for as long as he could remember.

The Chaplain, who was English, married them quietly with a sincerity which was very moving.

When they knelt for the blessing, Shana was sure that God was really blessing them.

The love which she and the Marquis had for each other was Divine.

When they returned to the Embassy the Ambassador and his wife drank their health and Lord Hallam said,

"I know that each of you has found the right person and it will therefore be impossible for you not to be exceedingly happy."

"I am *so* happy, Papa," Shana said. "I cannot believe – that this is all happening to me."

Still wearing her veil and holding her bouquet of lilies, they walked to the carriage.

They profusely thanked the Ambassador and his wife and Shana kissed her father again and again.

"Take care of yourself, Papa and I shall worry if you miss me when you return home."

"You will find your husband will give you an answer to that particular problem," Lord Hallam twinkled. "Do not think about coming home until you have explored Greece fully and perhaps seen your own face amongst all the Goddesses whose statues you will see."

"I do hope your wish comes true," Shana laughed.

As they drove away from the Embassy she slipped her hand into the Marquis's.

"How could you have thought of such a perfect wedding?" she asked. "Especially with Papa being there."

"That was a gift from the Gods," the Marquis replied. "And they have been very busy, as you know, my darling, looking after us ever since we first met in the *Rose and Crown*."

Shana grinned.

"Bob will be very surprised when he hears we are married."

"We will go and tell him the moment we get back, but we have a great many enthralling things to do first."

"Are we really going to Greece?"

"Where else could I take a Goddess?"

He raised her hand to his lips and kissed her fingers one by one.

Then he kissed the centre of her palm and she felt a little quiver of excitement run through her.

It seemed a long drive to the port of Ostia where the *Seashell* was waiting for them.

Curtis had gone ahead with the luggage so everyone on the ship already knew that they were married.

As they were piped aboard the crew showered them with rose petals and they walked into the Saloon to find flowers of every shape and colour in profusion.

As soon as they were aboard, the *Seashell* started to move.

The Marquis felt he would not really feel safe until they had passed out of the port and were in the open sea.

Shana had taken off her veil leaving the wreath of orchids in her hair.

She was still tidying herself in her cabin when a Steward knocked on the door and informed her that luncheon was ready.

She climbed upstairs to find that the Chef had excelled himself and each course was more delicious than the last.

It was however very difficult to think of food as she was so acutely conscious of her husband seated opposite her.

The expression in his eyes made her feel shy.

Luncheon was finished and the *Seashell* was steaming ahead at full speed.

"I have something to show you below," the Marquis said.

"I thought you might want us to watch the coast of Italy from the upper deck."

"We can do that later," the Marquis replied. "And I thought you would like to visit Venice before we sail on to Greece."

"All I hope is that there are plenty of books in your library about every place we are visiting. It is all so exciting and I do not want to miss anything either in what I see or what I read."

The Marquis smiled.

To her surprise they went into the Master Cabin.

As soon as they entered Shana realised that it was to be hers because it was decorated with flowers, which were arranged on the furniture and in every type of available vase.

"Is this to be my cabin?" Shana asked as she looked around.

"It is to be *ours*. Now my darling, I cannot wait any longer to kiss you and to tell you how much I love you."

He pulled her against him as he spoke.

Then as the ship swayed a little on the waves he sat down on the bed holding her like a child across his knees.

Then he was kissing her, kissing her as if for the first time, wildly, passionately.

Shana felt her heart leap upwards to him and her body melted into his.

"I love you. *I love you*," she whispered.

"As I love you," the Marquis murmured in a deep voice. "And my precious, I want to be closer to you than I am now and very much closer than I was last night."

Shana blushed and hid her face against his.

"I have so much to teach you about love," he continued, "and you have a great deal to teach me."

She looked up in surprise.

"How can I possibly do that?"

"I will tell you," he said. "And because it is precious and secret between us, I want you to get into bed."

He kissed her again.

Then as she felt her lips respond to his she wanted him to go on kissing and kissing her for ever.

He gently lifted her to one side.

"I will return very shortly," he said. "I have waited too long already. It seems like a thousand years."

He left the cabin as he spoke and Shana smiled.

Because she knew she must obey him she undressed.

While they had been having luncheon, Curtis had

unpacked her clothes and he had left her nightgown and dressing-gown on a chair.

She put on the nightgown trimmed with lace and blushed because it seemed rather transparent.

She had not been lying on the bed for more than a few minutes when the door opened and the Marquis entered.

The sunlight was pouring in through the portholes and the whole cabin glistened with the gold which shone in Shana's hair.

The Marquis threw his robe down onto a chair.

Climbing onto the bed he pulled Shana into his arms.

"My darling, my sweet, my loveliest one," he said. "This is really happening to us and I thought night after night when I slept here alone that my wish would never come true."

"Did you wish for me – in the fountain?" Shana asked.

"How could I have wished for anything else?" The Marquis was kissing her as he spoke.

At first very gently then more possessively, until his lips became even more passionate.

Shana felt her excitement turn into a flood of sensation she had never felt before.

It was like the sunshine coming through the portholes.

It was like the scent of thousands of beautiful flowers.

It seemed to invade her entire body and soul.

It was so exciting and so different from anything she had ever experienced, she could hardly believe it was true.

At the same time it was the most wonderful thing that had ever happened to her.

This was *love*, the love she had wished for and prayed for.

'I love you, I adore you,' she wanted to say but there was no need for words.

The Marquis was holding her closer and still closer.

They were both part of the sunshine and the glory of it made it impossible to think – only to feel.

As the Marquis made her his they were both in the burning heart of the sun.

They had found each other, as the Greeks believed, after years or perhaps centuries when they had been apart.

Now they were no longer two beings but one.

*

It was later in the afternoon when Shana, with her head on the Marquis's shoulder, asked,

"You have not yet told me, my wonderful husband, what you meant when you said I could – teach *you*."

The Marquis smiled.

"I have taught you, my darling, adorable little Goddess, a little about love and there is a great deal more for you to learn."

"It was – wonderful, too – wonderful for – words," Shana murmured.

"But you have to teach me," the Marquis continued, "how I can make the best of myself and therefore worthy of you. I know you are going to demand a great deal, but because I love you so completely, I will try to do what you ask of me."

Shana thought that no one could say anything more marvellous to her.

"You are also," he added, "in your innocence and your purity utterly different from any woman I have known. You have therefore, my darling, to teach me so much, which you know instinctively is pure and perfect and part of God Himself."

He paused for a moment.

"It is what I need and I know that you will give it to me and it is what you must give to our children."

He spoke so seriously and his words were so moving that Shana felt tears come into her eyes.

"I adore you," she sighed, "you are so magnificent yet so understanding."

"We understand each other," the Marquis told her, "because now we are inseparable. No one can ever part us and our journey to love is only just beginning."

Then he was kissing Shana once again.

They were enveloped in the light from the sun.

And at the same time in the Divine light which comes from God and is Love.

The Love which is Eternal and lasts forever.